MIND KEEPER

Some Monsters are Real

Derek Finn

frogsnotpigeons

Frogsnotpigeons

ISBN-13: 9798333379047
ISBN-10: 1477123456

Cover design by: frogsnotpigeons
Library of Congress Control Number: 2018675309
Printed in the United States of America

To my loved ones, whose unwavering support and wisdom have been my guiding light.
To my friends, who remind me to cherish the journey as much as the destination.
To all the seekers of knowledge, who believe in the mind's power to transform our lives.
May this book serve as a beacon of hope, guiding you toward a healthier, happier, and more mindful life.

With deepest gratitude and love,
Derek Finn

CONTENTS

Title Page

Copyright

Dedication

Introduction   1

Complexity of Dementia   6

A Letty Conversation   12

Alter Ego 1 Sarah Ryan: Emotion   16

Alter Ego 2 Alan Irvenko: Anger   22

Alter Ego 3 Letty Stark: Apophenia   33

Genetic Evolution   42

Religious Service   48

Life is Business   53

Conscious Transfer: Prototype 01   60

Anger Release   67

More Time   75

Time and the Mind   81

The Last Supper   86

The Age Gene   97

Splitting Personality   106

Religious Protocol   109

Reversing the Spiral   116

Who We Are   122

Live Forever   131

The Mind Keeper   136

Re-emergence   142

Separation   151

About The Author   157

Books By This Author   159

Mind Keeper   161

Mind Keeper
Derek Finn

AUGUST 6, 2024
DEREK FINN
frogsnotpigeons

INTRODUCTION

Although a fictitious story, the story is based on a real life character. I first met Letty Stark in October 2021, two years before she passed away in 2023. I still remember as she walked into the hotel foyer my initial surprise. She was a small demure of a woman with fine silver hair that appeared slightly bohemian. Her hair tied up to form a sort of bunch on the top of her head that kept her face clear. Her clothing reflecting fashion from a couple of decades ago in the form of a gray and purple check woolen suit and a 70s style blouse with oversized collars and a colorful scarf. She walked directly up to me faster than I expected for a person of age, as though with deliberate intent.

"Hello, I'm Letty Stark," she said with her right hand outstretched.

"Nice to meet you, Mrs. Stark," I reciprocated, standing to my feet promptly.

"Oh please, call me Letty. Or Alan, whatever is the more comfortable for you."

Not sure what to say, this caught me by surprise and I chose not to answer.

Letty deftly took a seat opposite me at the small lounge table and took some time to adjust the seat backwards and forwards until just right.

"Would you like a coffee, perhaps, or something else to drink?" I ventured.

"Perhaps a glass of still water, if not too much trouble."

I motioned to a server who promptly attended to Letty's needs and poured a glass of water from the bottle, deftly placing the bottle on the glass tabletop. Letty leaned forward and sipped ever so delicately from the small glass. All the while, she kept her attention focused on the water as though overly concentrating.

My first impression was how frail she looked. The skin on her face was coarse and wrinkled, reflecting her advanced age. In contrast, her eyes looked sharp and focused.

After a brief exchange of the usual platitudes that included the weather and traffic, the conversation turned quickly to the point of the meeting.

"Shall we begin?" asked Letty as she tilted her head position and looked up directly at me across the table.

"After all, time is exactly what we don't have."

In a world where the intricacies of the human mind often remain shrouded in mystery, 'Mind Keeper' emerges as a beacon of exploration, inviting readers into the complex and captivating world of Letty Stark and her multiple personality disorder.

Authored by Derek Finn, a retired biochemical engineer with a background in biotechnology, cell therapy, and applied psychology, this psychological fiction story weaves a tale that is as intellectually stimulating as it is emotionally gripping. Through the lens of his protagonist, Letty Stark, Finn takes us on a journey that delves deep into the realms of neuroscience, psychology, and the shadowy territories of the human psyche.

Letty Stark is not your typical heroine. Letty Stark presents herself as a composed and successful individual, navigating the corridors of her professional life with precision and control. Yet, beneath this facade lies a tumultuous inner world marked by psychopathic tendencies and Dissociative Identity Disorder (DID), a condition where multiple distinct identities coexist within a single individual. Each of Letty's personas is a testament to her fractured psyche, each vying for control, each a guardian of the different aspects of her personality and memories.

From the outset, 'Mind Keeper' immerses readers in the intricate web of Letty's mind. The narrative begins with a glimpse into her daily life, a seemingly ordinary existence marred by extraordinary challenges. Letty's condition, rooted in a traumatic past, manifests through various personas that emerge unpredictably, often triggered by stress or specific stimuli. These alter egos range from the nurturing and protective to the dangerously vengeful, creating a volatile and unpredictable internal landscape.

As Finn expertly unfolds Letty's story, he interlaces it with insights from his academic background in neuroscience and psychology. The novel does not merely depict the manifestations of DID, but delves into the underlying mechanisms that govern this complex disorder. Through detailed and nuanced descriptions, readers gain an understanding of how trauma, neural pathways, and psychological defenses interplay to create multiple identities within a single mind. Finn's background in applied psychology and neuroscience shines through as he explains these concepts with clarity and empathy, making the scientific aspects accessible without oversimplifying their complexity.

Interspersed within the story are short narratives that allude to the psychological aspects of mental illness relating to Letty's condition. These short narratives serve as both guides and mirrors, reflecting the real-world implications of

DID and offering a broad perspective on mental health. Their interactions with Letty are pivotal, shedding light on the therapeutic processes and ethical dilemmas involved in treating such a multifaceted disorder. These narratives also underscore the societal challenges faced by individuals with DID, from stigma to the struggle for acceptance and understanding.

The story of Letty Stark is not just a clinical case study; it is a riveting psychological thriller that presents more questions than it does answers. As Letty navigates her life, she becomes embroiled in a series of events that challenge her grip on reality.

Each twist and turn in the plot reveals more about her past and the origins of her multiple identities. Finn masterfully builds suspense, intertwining Letty's personal battles with external conflicts that mirror her internal chaos. The narrative momentum keeps readers on edge, drawing them deeper into the enigma of Letty's mind.

Perhaps one of the most interesting aspects of 'Mind Keeper' is its exploration of the ethical and philosophical questions surrounding identity and consciousness. Letty's journey forces readers to confront their own perceptions of normalcy and sanity. What does it mean to be a coherent self? How do we reconcile the different facets of our personalities? This book challenges us to look beyond the surface, to recognize the profound and often painful complexities that define human experience.

'Mind Keeper' serves as a poignant commentary on the human condition. Letty's struggle for self-understanding and integration mirrors the universal quest for identity and purpose. Her story is one of resilience and redemption, highlighting the strength of the human spirit in the face of overwhelming odds. Through Letty, Finn explores themes of trauma, healing, and the enduring hope for wholeness, making her journey a deeply resonant and inspirational tale.

In the end, Letty Stark's story is a mirror reflecting the fragmented nature of human consciousness. It reminds us we are all, in some ways, mind keepers—guardians of our thoughts, memories, and identities. Derek Finn's 'Mind Keeper' is more than just a novel; it is an invitation to explore the depths of the human mind, to understand the delicate interplay of mental health and identity, and to appreciate the intricate beauty of our inner worlds.

Welcome to the world of Letty Stark. Welcome to 'Mind Keeper'.

COMPLEXITY OF DEMENTIA

In the twilight of her life, Letty Stark's cognitive faculties started to betray her, heralding the inevitable onset of dementia that comes with age for all of us. Her considerable inherited financial wealth and connections granted her access to innovative scientific research, conducted in shadowy private laboratories that often-flouted ethical standards in pursuit of profit.

With a keen interest in understanding and manipulating the workings of the human brain, Letty delved into the realms of brain imaging technology, experimental psychotropic drugs, and cell & cene therapy. She hoped to find the key to unlock the extending of healthy life through a healthy mind.

The ancient brain amygdala and superior olivary cortex are nestled deep within the brain, and emerged as a focal point of Letty Stark's research. As the primal seat of emotions, the amygdala wields considerable influence over human behavior. Recent studies illuminated its perpetual conflict with the frontal cortex, the locus of rational decision-making. The superior olivary cortex (SOC) is a critical structure in the auditory pathway in the brainstem. It plays a key role in sound localization by processing auditory information from both ears. The SOC is divided into three main nuclei: the medial superior olive (MSO), the lateral superior olive (LSO), and the medial nucleus of the trapezoid body (MNTB). The MSO primarily detects interaural time differences, while the LSO is sensitive to interaural level differences. These functions are crucial for spatial hearing, allowing organisms to pinpoint the direction and distance of sounds in their environment. Essentially, the superior olivary cortex is part of the brain auditory system. It's why we look in a particular direction when we hear a loud sound. Sound location is detected by synthesizing sound in the olivary cortex via the auditory canals and offers a potential pathway to entraining low frequency signals directly to the brain.

Certain individuals exhibit impulsive brutality because they have a deficiency in serotonin, a chemical neurotransmitter crucial for assessing the consequences of one's actions. When the amygdala hijacks control from the frontal lobe, decision-making becomes impaired, paving the way for erratic behavior. However, it's likely that any biochemical imbalance in the brain could precipitate profound changes in behavior.

As an example of chemical imbalance, early analyzes of Letty's blood and urine samples revealed intriguing anomalies. While copper, zinc, and histamine levels appeared typical for her age, one result stood out markedly. Analysis of her samples showed elevated concentrations of pyroluria, a compound known to interfere with brain function.

Advocates of pyroluria suggest that the condition may lead to a variety of symptoms, including anxiety and panic attacks, mood swings, irritability and memory loss. Although not inherently indicative of a specific brain disorder, such unusually high levels are also commonly associated with psychiatric dysfunction and serve as early harbingers of cognitive decline. Notably, individuals exhibiting high levels of pyroluria often displayed symptoms similar to psychopathy, including dissociative identity disorder, uncontrollable rage, mood swings, photophobia, and memory lapses.

Letty, cognizant of her own test results, approached her condition with a pragmatic resolve. While not overly concerned by her diagnosis, she recognized the need for stringent measures to regulate her behavior. Adopting a lifestyle characterized by minimal stress, disciplined dietary habits, and above all, predictability.

With these control measures, she sought to stave off the tumultuous impulses lurking within her psyche. Yet deviations from this carefully crafted equilibrium invariably unleashed torrents of uncontrollable fury, punctuated by episodes of violence and subsequent amnesia. In these moments, Letty became a slave to her own neurochemical imbalances, her consciousness held hostage by primal urges beyond her control.

Aware that time was a dwindling commodity in her battle against the on-set of dementia, Letty harbored a profound dread of institutionalization.

The prospect of relinquishing her autonomy to the confines of a care facility loomed as a specter of unimaginable horror, compelling her to explore every avenue of resistance.

Reflecting on her life, Letty's aspirations soared to lofty heights, save for one glaring deficiency: her age depleting physical frailty versus the strength of youth.

Driven by an insatiable desire to reclaim the vigor of youth, Letty viewed the aging process as an adversary to be vanquished. This was her invisible enemy. Convinced that physical weakness was a mere impediment to be overcome, she immersed herself in a fervent quest for rejuvenation. Yet, as her fixation on physical prowess intensified, her psyche fragmented, giving rise to a cacophony of internal voices and personas, as is typical in dissociative personality disorders.

Bereft of her husband's stabilizing presence, Letty found

solace in the companionship of her alter egos, forging intimate bonds with figments of her own fractured consciousness.

Childhood experiences and parental influences exerted a profound imprint on Letty's adult psyche, shaping her worldview and driving her relentless, and selfish, pursuit of self-preservation. The story that follows chart's a fictitious Letty Stark's odyssey. A fictitious journey through the labyrinthine corridors of her mind as she wages a war against the ravages of time and the physical biological limitations imposed by aging.

Rooted in a biochemical imbalance that skewed her perception of reality, Letty's journey unfolds as a testament to the complex interplay between cognition, emotion, and morality.

For as long as she could remember, Letty found steadfast allies in the alter ego forms of two particular alternate personalities as Alan and Sarah. Embodiments of her innermost thoughts and desires.

As a child, Letty's parents and teachers referred to the characters as imaginary friends to be made fun of. However, to Letty, they transcended mere figments of her imagination, assuming corporeal form in the crucible of her fractured psyche.

Alan, as a male alter ego, represented her dark side, the physicality, anger and rage. He was her strength and gave Letty the capability constrained only by her cognitive ability to control her anger. The softer Sarah character represented a caring and emotional side of Letty. Yet, to outsiders, they remained elusive specters, manifestations of Letty's profound disconnect from the world around her.

It had been five years since Letty and her team had embarked on their ground-breaking project at the privately funded and secretive Mind Keeper Cognition Laboratory. Their goal: to identify the source of consciousness and harvest the mind to enable life beyond the frailty of a failing physical body. To decode and harness the brain's predictive abilities to extend the quality of aging life. They had made significant strides and the culmination of their efforts was now unfolding before her eyes.

The brain, and specifically consciousness, Letty had determined was the ultimate prediction machine. It was a concept that had fascinated her since before her early days as a neuroscience student. She remembered reading about how the brain constantly generated hypotheses about the world, predicting sensory input and adjusting its models based on the discrepancies between expectation and reality. It was this continuous feedback loop that allowed humans to navigate their environments with such precision and efficiency.

As she zoomed in on a particular cluster of neurons, Letty reflected on the various experiments they had already conducted. One of the most revealing had involved monitoring the brain activity of subjects as they performed a simple task: catching a basketball. High-speed cameras tracked the ball's trajectory, while electrodes recorded the internal brain neural responses. What they discovered was astounding. Even before the ball had left the thrower's hand, the brain was already simulating multiple paths, preparing the body to react to each potential scenario.

"The anticipatory signals are off the charts," Letty had exclaimed during the initial review of the data.

"It's like the brain is running a continuous stream of 'what if' simulations, playing out pre-determined patterns to predict response?"

Her alter egos were, of course, in agreement, sharing Letty's enthusiasm.

"And it's not just reacting to the environment; it's predicting it. Every sensory input is a piece of data that refines its model of the world."

The internal mind collective watched on in unison as the various parts of the brain responded to stimulation and electrical signals that crossed neural pathways over both sides of the brain. They realised that consciousness was not a physical aspect of the organ brain but more of a phenomenon of the brain's output in electro chemical signalling.

Letty adjusted the hologram to display the prefrontal cortex. This area, she knew, was crucial for higher-order predictions. It was here the brain synthesized information from various sensory modalities, integrating experiences and contextual cues to generate predictions about future events.

"Let's run the simulation again," she said aloud, her voice breaking the silence of the otherwise empty lab.

The hologram shifted, animating the neural pathways as data flowed through them. The simulation depicted a person walking through a crowded streetscape. As the virtual figure moved, the prefrontal cortex lit up, constantly updating its predictions based on the ever-changing sensory input. A sudden movement by another virtual pedestrian on the opposite trajectory — triggered a cascade of predictions, each pathway representing a different potential outcome. The figure adjusted its course seamlessly, avoiding a collision without conscious thought.

"This is it," Letty whispers to her alternative egos.

"This is how we navigate the world—by predicting future actions before they happen."

But as the silent conversation progressed, Letty couldn't shake a nagging thought. The brain's predictive power was a double-edged sword. While it allowed for incredible adaptability, it also meant that errors in prediction could have serious consequences. Misjudgments, biases, and overconfidence could lead to catastrophic outcomes. She also wondered about the longer term reliability of predicting outcomes before they happen. Is it possible that people who predict their future maladies of diabetes or early onset dementia are the creators of this reality?

Each of the egos of Letty wondered in silence at the meaning of consciousness and the prediction function inferred through brain imaging. The specter of mental illness, dementia, and the question of how could three consciousness in one mind operate facing the absolute certainty of age related frailty of the human condition itself?

A LETTY CONVERSATION

As a sixteen-year-old student, Letty Stark sat in the cozy surrounds of the school library at Saint Paul's Community School in her hometown of Waterford in the South of Ireland. She stared down at the chessboard, pondering her opponent's next move.

"Dear Letty, if I may call you that, you are so intense. It's completely natural to worry about life and what might come," said the English teacher, Mr. Hartree, his eyes glinting like sunlight on frosted morning grass.

Mr. Hartree made his move. A black pawn moving one step closer towards the preserved neat row of opposing white pawns.

"Of course, you are worried about your future and what you will do with your life. But you can be anything you want, Letty. You just set your mind on what you want to do and do it. How is that not exciting?"

"Maybe. I suppose it could be," answers Letty in a slightly unconvincing tone.

"Your entire life is an opportunity waiting for you to take it."

"My entire life?"

"You can be anything you want to be if you apply yourself now. Live anywhere you want, perhaps a nice warm climate, meet nice people. Isn't that an exciting thought?"

Letty pushed her knight forward, leaping over Mr. Hartree's pawn.

It was hard not to compare Mr. Hartree to her alcoholic father, who treated Letty as a disappointment. An unexpected arrival into his life that had complicated his drinking social life without consideration. An expense to be endured, and an unplanned disruption to his boring and mediocre life.

For instance, when Letty turned sixteen, her father arranged a part-time job for her, delivering newspapers to the nearby council estate. He insisted that someone like Letty was not privileged and that school education was overrated. Letty was so enraged that on her first, and last day, she took a lighter and set fire to the entire stack of newspapers, earning the scorn of the entire housing estate, who missed their weekly betting results. Her father made his dissatisfaction known to Letty by catching her beloved 6-month-old kitten named Snowy and throwing the poor animal over their garden fence into the path of busy traffic. Snowy had no chance of survival, and Letty blocked the memory from her mind.

"Don't you just *hate* the damp and cold," added Mr. Hartree with emphasis.

Like all of us, Mr. Hartree was an aging man. Perhaps late fifties or early sixties with a receding hairline and thick-rimmed glasses balanced on his nose. Little tufts of hair grew from his nose and ears like wild weeds that needed to be tended to. Despite his age, Mr. Hartree gave his time willingly to pupils in his care. He felt attuned to the younger generations' wavelength, even going as far as 'high fiving' students, as though showing an understanding of modern traditions with his students.

"Damp and cold don't always go together," Letty told him. "The moon is freezing and very dry at the same time."

"Is it? That sounds fantastic–you should go there. You would fit in great there, I am sure. But I also hear not the best place to raise children," he smiled coyly.

"Mmm... maybe not. I don't think it would be far enough away from here."

"Maybe you could be a crew member on the International Space Station orbiting the earth for months at a time? Or perhaps a super small neuroscientist who travels deep into the brains of others on a miniature craft?"

Letty smiles. "Only if I'm the navigator. Do they have access to social media and fast broadband speed inside a brain?"

Mr. Hartree removed his thick-rimmed glasses and cleaned the lens on his shirtsleeve before delicately placing them back on his nose. "Now you're thinking. See, you can be anything you set your mind to".

Letty's attention drifted, and she glanced out the window to her side. She recognized the old tea lady walking ever so slowly across the courtyard path and thought for a moment of life expectancy for old people.

Surely, she can't live much longer, she mused to herself. Her father had passed away much younger than the tea lady, but perhaps it was because the tea lady still had a functioning liver.

Letty did not enjoy school much and outside of her imaginary friends, had a small circle of 'real world' friends. Mostly binding together for self-protection from the other students who classed Letty as a geek and a target for ridicule.

'Wacko' or 'Weird' were common names.

"My father told me once that I am wasting time at school and should spend more time at home helping with the washing and cleaning and cooking. Society believes that people like us have a pre-determined life. Get married, council house, have kids and be a good stay-at-home parent does not require education."

"Well, far be it from me to contradict your dad's wisdom. Perhaps there is more to Letty Stark than being a stay-at-home parent. There are many choices you can make that will change how your life will be. Perhaps our lives are not pre-destined, and we choose the life we want to live. Letty Stark, I am sure that you can be anything that...."

And it was then that the fire alarm sounded. A deafening sound wailed that hurt normal hearing.

"Dang, another false alarm evacuation," said Mr. Hartree, "We should go."

Letty instinctively turned in her seat and slipped on her plastic rain jacket. As she got to her feet, she tipped her head sideways and tightly pursed her lips as if to stop her tongue from falling out. A small 'royal like' wave of her hand to signal a silent thanks without words, she swung open the office door to leave for the front gate.

ALTER EGO 1 SARAH RYAN: EMOTION

A s a young girl, Letty had always been sensitive to the emotional frequency of those around her. She could pick up on the slightest changes in tone or body language, and she often found herself overwhelmed by the intensity of other people's feelings.

It wasn't until she was a teenager that Letty realized that her sensitivity to emotions was a gift. She discovered the pattern of words in poetry and beauty in nature. She found she had a talent for expressing in words the complex and nuanced emotions she saw in the unhappy world around her.

Letty's heightened sense of awareness carried into nature and the world around her and she felt she could sense the background frequency to nature. The Earth's natural frequency of 7.83Hz. Although not fully understanding why, Letty was tuned to this geometry of nature.

She felt her entire body influenced by the constant, almost combative frequency of moon and tides, of the sun and stars, and of the cycle of change controlled by an invisible yet perceivable force of nature. Letty expressed this emotional side of her personality in the form of an alternate character represented through Letty as Sarah Ryan.

Letty shared her poetry interests online, and she quickly gained a following of people who appreciated her unique perspective on life. Her poems were raw and honest, filled with a deep sense of empathy and compassion.

One day, Letty received an imaginary, unsolicited email from a woman named Sarah Ryan. Letty created an internal soap opera that told her that Sarah had stumbled upon Letty's poetry on social media, and one of Letty's poems had deeply moved her about loss and grief. Sarah shared she had lost her father to alcohol and her mother more recently to brain disease. She expressed her feeling of inadequacy to do anything as her mother suffered pre-mature aging brought on by dementia. Similar to Letty, Sarah talked about her own disappointment in life and the uncertainty of the future.

Each appeared to share a bond in the others desperation for something different that connected them both.

Letty responded to Sarah's email, and the two of them struck up an imaginary conversation. They talked about loss and grief, about how pain could sometimes feel overwhelming and all-consuming. Letty shared some of her own experiences with loss, and Sarah found comfort in knowing that she wasn't alone in her feelings.

Over the next few months, Letty and Sarah continued to correspond privately. They talked about everything from their favourite books to the challenges of growing up, the fear of parenting and where life will take them. But at the heart of their conversations was a deep sense of connection, a shared understanding of the power of sentiment and emotion. The connection was so strong that it felt like they were the same person talking. Of course, the reality was that they were the same person but simply spoke as separate minds within the mind of the other.

One day, Sarah surprised Letty by telling her she had written her own poetry. She had always loved to read, but she had never considered herself a writer. But something about Letty's poetry had inspired her, and she had put her feelings into words.

Letty's heart filled with joy upon hearing this, and she enthusiastically encouraged Sarah to continue writing. She knew first-hand the healing power of words, and she believed Sarah had a gift that deserved to be shared with the world.

Months passed, and Letty and Sarah continued to correspond. They talked about their dreams and fears, about the beauty and the pain of the world around them. And all the while, Sarah continued to write poetry, slowly but surely, building up the confidence to share her work with others.

Then, one day, Sarah sent Letty a link to a blog she had started. The blog was a collection of Sarah's poems, and it was filled with raw emotion and deep feeling that Letty recognized immediately as the work she had previously shared with Sarah. Letty was happy Sarah had finally found the courage to share her gift with the world, and Letty was overjoyed to see the impact that Sarah's words were having on others.

However, as though an approaching storm in the distance, Letty also sensed a new and dark jealous emotion deep down inside her.

As time passed and months turned into years, Sarah and Letty continued to correspond with each other. Letty saw Sarah as a younger version of herself, even considering Sarah as part of her consciousness.

Letty realized that her gift wasn't just about feeling emotions. It was about using those emotions to connect with others, to help them see they weren't alone in their struggles and their pain. She had helped Sarah find her soft and caring voice, and in doing so, she had discovered the true power of sentiment.

"I agree with the sentiment," she read from the cell phone screen a message from Sarah.

"What does that mean?" was the message back.

The silence that comes from a nonresponse to a text message hangs in the air between them. Staring at the small screen, waiting for the small dots that say someone is responding. But not this time.

No response should be enough, but it never is. Hanging on for something, a message that's not coming from someone who is not there.

Letty's rage clouds grew inside her silently at the none response on the screen. She sighed deeply at the disappointment. The specter of another personality was rising inside.

That sinking emptiness when you know for sure that you are alone. Loneliness is a deep feeling from the pit of the stomach and into your mind. It closes down rational thought and puts the mind into a spiral of despair. Emotions that come from a deep sense of loss.

It's a loss that is self-created, a combination of what you had, and what your mind tells you that you are going to miss out on in the future. Letty's rage storm came and went like an ebbing tide, following the pre-determined pattern of the moon across the night sky.

As the minutes ticked by, the silence on the other end of the screen became deafening.

For Letty, every passing moment seemed to stretch on for an eternity, each one more agonizing than the last. The hope that had been flickering within slowly extinguished, leaving behind a hollow emptiness that seemed to consume every inch of her being.

Letty and Sarah knew in their heart of hearts that a relationship of on-line messaging each other was not sustainable. That this silence was the ultimate confirmation of what they had been trying to deny for so long. But knowing didn't make it any easier. In fact, it only made it worse.

Letty thought to herself, how loneliness is a funny thing? It can make you feel you're the only person in the world, even when you're surrounded by others in your own head. It can make you question everything you thought you knew about yourself and your life. It can take hold of you and refuse to let go, no matter how hard you try to fight it.

And that's exactly what was happening. The emotions swirling around inside of them were too much to bear. The thought alone of losing one registered a pain that was just too great to contemplate. They felt like they were drowning in a sea of their own sadness, unable to find their way back to the surface.

But slowly, ever so slowly, they all realized something. They were still here. They were still alive, still breathing, still capable of feeling. And this meant there was hope.

Hope for a future that was different, yes. One that didn't depend on the person on the other end of the screen. But hope. Hope for a life that was full of love and joy and all the things they had missed for so long.

It was a hard realization to come to. It meant letting go of the past, of what could have been. But it also meant embracing the present, and all the possibilities that lay ahead.

So, Letty took a deep breath on behalf of herself and Sarah, wiped away their tears, and moved forward. It wasn't easy, and it wasn't quick. But little by little, they rebuilt their constructed life. They discovered new shared interests, new hobbies, new passions.

They discovered that there was so much more to life than they had ever realized.

And as time went on, the pain of the silent moments faded. It didn't disappear entirely, of course. There would always be a part of them that would remember and each of them shared a same space in one mind. It no longer controlled them, no longer consumed them.

Instead, they could look forward with hope and optimism. They could find joy in the small moments, and to appreciate the people and experiences making their life worth living. They could let go of what had been and embrace what was yet to come.

And in that psychological virtual embrace, they found peace. A peace that came not from the absence of pain, but from the acceptance of it. A peace that came from knowing that they were strong enough to survive, and they had so much to live for.

Both Letty and Sarah knew deep down they were the same person and would always be together in conscious thought. Their shared consciousness predicted a life together where each personality would materialize and live their dreams as one.

Night-time was always the worst for Letty. Her darkness dreams continued to grow stronger inside her mind until her third alternate personality introduced himself to Letty and Sarah.

ALTER EGO 2 ALAN IRVENKO: ANGER

Fear and hopelessness were the only things that the persona of Alan had remembered throughout his youth. A side of him inherited from Letty. Raised by a violent alcoholic stepfather, and a mother who was indifferent to her husband's cruelty towards her children. He blamed them both equally.

Alan's younger siblings suffered the most. By the time Alan reached his early teens, he had learned not to stay around the house and spent his time on the street corner with the jolly boy crew. Staying out as late as possible was the target, regardless of the weather or who else was hanging about. Despite there being no one else out. It was preferable to be alone in the rain than at home listening to the ranting from a drunken coward of a man.

At least most of the time. Other times, Alan couldn't bear to think of his younger siblings in the house alone, in case of what might happen. Alan regularly intervened on behalf of his siblings and accepted the verbal and physical abuse. Feeling the pain of a leather belt across the back, or the slap of a shovel-sized hand across the face so hard that his skin tingled and eventually became numb. It didn't matter, there was no escape, and Alan accepted his lot, sending his mind as distant as his imagination could take him.

Over time, a rage grew deep inside the mind of the teenager. It grew inside him until someone, or something, released it; and when it did eventually surface, it would explode.

Usually, this rage was blind and totally uncontrolled. Alan's mind blanked in these raging explosions where he would attack his release target with such a violence that it shocked onlookers.

He could not control these episodes and only stopped when someone else would drag him off his victim or back to reality. Like a flashing light somewhere in the distance, Alan's consciousness in the imaginary form of Letty Stark, would gradually return to him, and a wave of remorse flooded his confusion as he saw his stepfather's image look back at him from a nearby reflective surface.

Are we a product of our past? Does our upbringing decide who we are today?

Like Letty, Alan also asked himself these questions many times. He shuddered at the thought he could ever be the person who he resented and despised the most. With his head on the pillow, he would stare at the ceiling and imagine patterns in the swirls of white ceiling emulsion, trying to make out a non-existent message. Looking for a pattern that was not there. Imagination let him escape a miserable life and block out the sounds of violence that permeated from downstairs and into the young boy's life.

And from this form of mind escapism, Alan's imagination became a trait that developed over the years to become a formidable defense mechanism. Of course, Alan was aware of the internal presence of his softer and creative egos in Sarah and Letty, but chose to mostly ignore this emotional side. Preferring strength over emotion.

Violence Over Empathy.

We are not determined by our past; he would mutter to himself repeatedly.

Like a mantra, it echoed in his mind, over and over, until he felt the frontal cerebral cortex pulse in his head at a single beat low frequency.

Despite spending so much time in his imagination, supported by Letty and Sarah, Alan eventually did very well at school and had a keen interest in reading, geometry, mathematics, and language. This was despite the homemade torn shirt collars and bruises that came from being dragged around and thrown against doors and walls. Long sleeves hid the fingerprint marks on his skin of abuse, and a large class size enabled him to hide in the back row. His wide grin hid reality, and he sheltered behind a sarcastic humor not always appreciated by those around him.

Despite the academic flair, and against the powerful persuasion of a respected and interested teacher, by the age of 17, Alan had already left school and, like Letty, decided that his new escape plan was to get as far away from home as possible. The destination didn't matter. It didn't matter what language they spoke. It was away, and that's all that mattered.

Besides the astute counseling teacher, one or two other schoolteachers intervened at this point and called to the family home. However, it was too little too late and Alan had set his mind to escape.

And not just in his imagination.

As hard as he tried, the deep-seated rage and bitterness seemed to follow young Alan. He knew how to survive and lived a semi-street life that became his education. Now and then, this blistering rage exploded to the surface, and he would hit the self-destruct button option. Spiraling out of control, until his mind had vented.

He could find trouble easily and felt a strange satisfaction searching for danger on dark streets that others avoided. A beating by a much larger and stronger opponent gave his internal torment a strange sense of relief. The bruising reminded him of who he was and where he came from. He took solace in this pain and the markings on his skin as a badge of honor for who he was.

As the years went by, the street gangs he was drawn to influenced Alan. The misplaced camaraderie and the sense of belonging made him feel like he was a part of something more than just him. Almost like the surrogate family of Sarah and Letty living in his mind.

The misplaced admiration for his selfish, uncaring attitude fueled him into more reckless behavior that made Alan seek danger. His natural intelligence and imagination brought him a certain success that he used to his advantage.

Alan wasn't hungry; he wasn't desperate; he found work when he needed it and did only what he wanted. This callous attitude attracted all sorts, who mistakenly took this confidence as borderline arrogance.

But Alan moved in circles around influential people. He shared the interests of Letty Stark in neuroscience and his brain was fascinated with the success of others. Although he knew he wasn't one of them, he was attracted to the influential circle of decision makers. The powerful who controlled and influenced the lives of others.

The invisible chip on Alan's shoulder kept him at a distance from others and followed him like a dark shadow. But eventually, Alan learned to control his deep rage and kept himself in check most of the time. But the self-destruct and reset buttons were never far away.

One hand on the button, always.

Alan moved around as though looking to escape his past. Of course, there is nowhere far enough away to escape the past, and it always likes to remind us of the same. However, now in his early twenties, Alan was steady and could hold down a job. At least for a couple of months. The attraction to the most elite decision makers, the influence on other people's lives, the certain correctness and mutual respect, intrigued the young Alan.

One of the more unusual attractions in Alan's orbit of the influential was the older woman character, who presented as Letty Stark. Alan found this mother figure of a woman fascinating, and he looked up to and secretly admired her.

Despite her advanced age, she was intellectually very capable. Letty showed the same interest in the young Alan and instantly recognized the dark behavioral pattern of a troubled mind. Her interest in Alan extended to sharing with him career opportunities at her company, and a mentor-mentee relationship had developed between the odd couple over multiple years.

Late one evening, Alan kicked off his shoes and sat down on his dilapidated sofa following a long day in the office. Catching up on the lives of others, he doom scrolled through his phone containing the millions of attention-seeking media volunteers, who shared their life with anyone who was remotely interested. Alan was looking for the unexpected in his small world screen of Tik-Tok.

And then something unexpected happened.
Someone was ringing the doorbell. Dringg.... Dringg.....

Alan wondered if he should answer, or perhaps if he waited long enough, the unexpected and unwanted presence at his door might just leave. The second door bell ring answered his thoughts loudly.

Alan fastened up a couple of buttons on his shirt to make himself look more presentable, and discovered that the person at the door was an older woman that he instantly recognized. It was Letty Stark.

She was small in demeanor and dressed in old-fashioned clothes, perhaps like old people do, clutching a small bag as though her life depended on it. But she had sharp eyes that looked like she could see through people.

Alan looked the old woman up and down, momentarily surprised. The contrast between the pair made him uneasy as he moved his weight to one leg and crossed his knee, while using one arm to hang from his front door. This only made him look more uneasy and his shirt lifted from his belt, drooping over his trouser pocket. For a moment, he forgot his loneliness-inspired depression in a meaningless universe. It was good to see her in physical presence.

"Mrs. Stark," he said, sounding concerned. "What are you doing here and out so late?"

Letty appeared to be leaning slightly forward, more than usual, like she was about to topple in through the door at any moment. Her eyes didn't look up at Alan, but focused on his wayward, untidy shirt.

"It's good to see you too," she said in a mumbled, low tone.

"You look like a walking jumble sale."

When she had spoken to him at work, she always sounded authoritative and fully alert, but now her voice sounded frail and apathetic.

Although Alan had spoken with Letty in his mind many times, he had somehow forgotten how old and frail the woman was. Letty raised her wrinkled hand slowly, extending it towards Alan. Intuitively, Alan took his arm off the door and accepted the offered hand, leading her while supporting her slight frame into the small dark hallway. At the same time, he noticed the scent of old people but ignored it as a mark of manners.

"I think she's dead. We may have killed her," said Letty without lifting her gaze.

"What?" he exclaimed. Not sure he heard correctly.

"She was lying very still on the ground, and there was a lot of blood. There was nothing I could have done Alan. I'm sorry."

Alan's dark emotional center switched on and his smile

dropped as he bent forward to bring his face closer to the same level as Letty. In doing so, he noticed the blood drops on Letty's shoes, and his mind froze as he tried to process what his senses were receiving.

Letty instantly turned her head for the first time and looked directly into the eyes of Alan. She felt the coldness of his dark stare.

"I need you, Alan."

"Er.. need me for what, Mrs. Stark?"

"You are part of my consciousness survival. I need your strength and youth to live on through me."

The sound of an object crashing to the hard floor broke the moment. Alan instantly looked to his feet, where he saw his mobile phone screen blinking back, still showing some teenage latest dance craze. He shook his head from side to side, to wake himself, and realized he was still on the old worn-out sofa, having drifted off to sleep.

Startled into being awake, Alan looked around the small box room that loomed out from a gray semi-darkness and wondered at the meaning of his dream. The curtain on the partially open window fluttered slightly in the early morning breeze.

It was quiet outside, and the neon street lights cast an alien glow of orange against the glass. Alan placed a hand on each corner of the small window ledge and stared out at the dusky street in the pale half light. He wondered if everyone else in the world was still awake.

At that moment, he felt a shiver. Alan took a deep breath of the refreshing morning air flowing through the slightly ajar window. He raised his head to admire the silver clouds drifting across the dark sky, catching fleeting glimpses of the stars peeking through the cloudy veil.

I must be awake anyway; he thought. He turned and picked up clothes from the floor and quickly put them on, followed by a pair of trainers. Grabbing his keys, he closed the small room door behind him and quickly headed down the wooden stairs and exited the front door of the bedsit. He made a final adjustment to his zipper and walked away from the door, as though with some yet unknown purpose.

Alan found himself consumed by the same clouds of rage and anger that Letty had encountered earlier in the day. He had already decided to find where danger was hiding. This included the town's darkest corners on the infamous streets to avoid.

As he turned one of these street corners in the still dark morning, Alan came across what he was looking for. A group of seven or eight delinquents hanging on a street corner. The loud talk and shouting confirmed alcohol intoxication or drugs or both. Alan swaggered purposely towards the group, hands clenched in hoody pockets and head down. A deliberate and intentional walk into a fix of violence.

Some hours later, Alan was back at his bedsit door. Turning the small yale key in the lock, he entered the communal hall and double-stepped back up the wooden stairs to his private box room door and his own space. He flopped down on the stained blue sofa, and after adjusting the cushions, stared at the ceiling. Reaching to the floor, Alan's hand searched and found the bottle of vodka still lying where it was left from the previous night. He unscrewed the cap and drank hard, the clear liquid that forced him to grimace as the strength of alcohol hit the back of his throat. It also numbed the pain that he now felt in his ribs and his scraped knuckles.

In his alcohol infused stupor, Alan's mind drifted into reflection where he did not want to go. Sending his thoughts back to his troubled youth. He consoled himself with how much his life had changed over the years. He thought back to his childhood and the constant fear and violence that had plagued his youth. The pain, the anger, the hopelessness, and the fear had all been a part of his daily existence. Poor Snowy–the small, innocent childhood memory of his white kitten unexpectedly flashed through his mind for a fleeting moment. A past he had broken free from, to rise above it all, and build a life for himself.

Poor Snowy, he deep sighed out loud.

Alan's mind wandered to happier times and his early years on the streets. The Jolly Boy crew, who had been his refuge from the violence and abuse of his home life, had taught him to be tough and self-reliant. They had shown him that there was a different way to live outside of the narrow confines of his abusive family life. He had spent his teenage years on the streets surviving any way he could, and slowly building a sense of purpose and direction.

But even in a drunken haze, Alan knew he needed to change his life. He couldn't keep living like this forever. He wanted more; Alan wanted to be more.

Despite the difficulties of his upbringing, he had always been a smart kid, and he soon discovered that he had a talent for learning that he put to beneficial effect under the odd stewardship of his mind mentor Letty Stark.

Letty was an odd old bird but had been a true inspiration to Alan. She had recognized his potential from the early days and had helped him to develop it. Letty had seen past his tough exterior and had understood the pain and suffering that lay beneath it. She had given him a chance when no one else would, and she had helped him to find a purpose and a direction in life.

Alan smiled almost embarrassingly, as he thought about the friendship that had developed between them. Such an unlikely pairing. In his mind, Letty had become like a surrogate mother to him, and he had learned so much from her. She had taught him about life, about business, and the power of kindness and compassion. She had shown him that there was a different way to live, one that didn't involve violence and rage as the only solution. In comparison, Sarah Ryan was an alter ego that Alan was not as close to. He thought of her creativity as pointless in a cruel and angry world that was his domain. However, he also knew that both of them were a part of him. Equally, that he was part of them.

As Alan sat on his couch, lost in thought, his phone rang. It was a voice he recognised as Sarah Ryan, calling to tell him that

Letty had passed away earlier that night. Alan was devastated but also confused. It was only hours ago that he had dreamt of Letty at his door with bloodstains on her shoes. He still felt the conscious presence of Letty inside him. He knew Letty was part of his conscious being and she would want him to keep going, to keep striving for excellence, and to never give up.

And so, with a confused mind, Alan swung his legs to the floor and rose from his couch. If Letty's bodily representation had passed on, then how could he still sense the presence of Letty in his mind?

Showered, shaved, and dressed, he made his way down the narrow bedsit stairs to the street outside. He knew he had a lot to live up to, but he also knew that he had the strength and the determination to make it happen. He had come so far already, and he wasn't about to give up now.

As he walked into the workplace office, he looked around at his colleagues, and he smiled. He felt somehow different. Empowered. Not sure why, he knew he was a different person, that he had overcome so much, and that he could achieve great things. He felt he had found his purpose in life, and he was going to do everything in his power to fulfil it.

In some small way, Alan realized he was no longer a victim of his past. Letty had helped him take control of his life, and he had made it his own. He had broken free from the cycle of violence and rage that had once defined him, and he had become something greater and something more. He had become a survivor, a fighter, and a leader. And Letty constantly reminded him that there was no limit to what he could achieve if he put his mind to it.

Alan swung his desk chair slightly as he sipped on his single shot Americano from the coffee machine. Careful not to stain the crisp white shirt under his dark blue suit. To his right, overlooking his desk, his mind saw the hanging wall picture images of his mentor Letty Stark and her youngest adopted protégé, Sarah Ryan. Sarah was the last connection to Letty and also the closest to Alan. Alan sat back in his chair momentarily reflecting on his mind friend Letty Stark. The personified version of balance, logic, and practicality in his life.

ALTER EGO 3 LETTY STARK: APOPHENIA

L etty Stark was born in 1940 and died in 2023. Letty's husband had died in 2001 some twenty years before Letty and she had not remarried. Although she had no children of her own, Letty had an imaginary relationship with a much younger woman she met through social media as part of a grief support group following her husband's death. Perhaps as a grief coping mechanism, Letty created elaborate soap opera episodes to describe her imaginary friends to appease her own mind and that of others. Sarah Ryan was a good friend and companion to Letty and the pair had developed a strange, but mutually beneficial, stepmother daughter relationship that comforted them both. Eventually, Letty brought Sarah into her work life and Sarah willingly assumed the role. Letty informed her real-world colleagues that she had funded university study for Sarah in bio-medical science and post study, had taken Sarah into her research work as part of a research doctoral. Of course, none of this was true. Letty simply created the stories in her mind to explain to others an easier version of her reality.

Sarah treated Letty Stark like a mother carer role. Not unlike Alan, both women shared a deep interest in science and shared many hours of conversation on healthy aging and prediction theory that became an obsession for them both.

When they were younger, both enjoyed poetry writing and willingly shared back-and-forth correspondence through social media and text messaging regularly. Often, this lighthearted messaging included Alan in a group chat forum. As Letty grew older and less firm, Sarah accepted an additional role of caregiver to her step-mother.

Sarah knew Letty was prone to helping others less fortunate. Perhaps it was because she had no children of her own that Letty appeared to search out substitute stepchildren to support. Sarah knew herself as one of Letty's alter personalities and appreciated everything the old woman had done for her. Sarah also knew she was not the only alter ego in Letty's life and had met the personality of Alan Irvenko on several previous occasions and shared conversations. Although they had not connected on a personal level, they had the shared interests of work and, of course, the shared alter ego of Letty Stark. However, although physically fit for her age, Letty could not offset the effects of memory loss brought on by the cruelness of age related dementia. This disease of the brain is unselective, unforgiving, and wreaks havoc on the brain of the unsuspecting host.

It would be true to say that Letty's endeavors in mind health focused primarily on the prevention of her own cognitive decline, and yes, she had some success.

Like many sociopaths, Letty had a fascination with patterns. This is the unique human behavior that sets humans apart from other mammals. It is precisely this marvelous ability to identify patterns in the information submitted continuously by our senses that is the beginning of reasoning and abstract thinking.

Our savage ancestors from the distant past survived by the ability to recognize and predict the behavior patterns or migration paths of the animals that provided food. This inherited trait subsequently became a genetic marker that carried through evolution. The brain that could not identify the repetitive pattern of animal migration, or connections to seasons, quickly became the food of a predator that could. Eventually, failed genetic markers became obsolete and died out, favoring the pattern readers of modern humans today.

Letty Stark, supported by her compassionate alter ego, Sarah, spent a large part of her life obsessed with nature's fractural patterns. The more sophisticated and ever-more subtle, the better.

It is pattern recognition in music, mathematics and poetry that gives great aesthetic enjoyment to those that recognize the pattern of rhythm. There is a fine line between perceiving subtle patterns and experiencing Apophenia, a cognitive condition where one sees patterns that are not actually there. Apophenia is a condition that is closely associated with schizophrenia. Apophenia is also associated with conspiracy theorists and with individual brilliance, leading to narcissistic behavior of the alter ego filled by Alan Irvenko.

Not surprisingly, modern humans all seem to be on the verge of Apophenia to varying degrees. The brain that can identify the pattern of the tides and the relationship to the moon may also connect the traverse of a distant fiery comet across the universe to the birth of a new king, or the outcome of an upcoming election.

Letty's exquisite mind saw patterns in people's behaviors, in nature, in situational contexts, and she was thrilled to predict outcomes. She believed that the human brain was the ultimate prediction machine that took information from the outside world via the senses and internally created the life we experience. Combining patterns and prediction, Letty believed that a celestial event of a passing comet that occurred every eighty three years was also the marker of her birth and of her death. Her challenge was to offset cognitive decline before she reached her physical-biological end date and to define consciousness to take advantage of her younger self alter characters–Alan and Sarah.

Letty understood that the human brain could define patterns through information collected by the senses. It was exactly this ability to recognize familiar patterns in unfamiliar situations that gave humans reasoning, analogy, problem-solving, and abstract thought.

Patterns give us pleasure, and our minds are uniquely developed to live and survive in patterns. Seasons, tidal change, star formations, clouds, language, music, mathematics, and physics are all forms of patterns in the world we live in that many of us take for granted around us.

To keep the mind active for as long as possible, Letty used her financial independence provided by her late husband's inheritance and company resources to support her mind-enhancement endeavors. This work activity focused on pattern identification as a modality to predict, and where necessary, influence preferred outcomes. Applications of brainwave entrainment using binaural beats and low frequency signals adapted from nature itself provided potential behavior influences that Letty Stark was sure could enhance healthy aging.

As Letty reflected, she thought about how history showed prediction and patterns that could help in our own life.

In 585 BC, there was a solar eclipse. The narrow band of total darkness caused by the moon passing across the face of the sun cast a perfect shadow over the Greek island of Mellitus. Although not unique by itself, and based on historical record for the time, this was the first eclipse that was predicted accurately. Thales of Mellitus calculated the moon would pass across the face of the sun, creating a shadow on the Earth on that day, that month of that year. This narrow swath of darkness passes over a small section of Earth only once every 359 to 400 years, so to predict this pattern for the time was amazing.

Related to pattern identification, Sacred Geometry is the philosophy behind geometrical patterns that naturally occur in nature. The concept is as old as life itself and dates back to ancient human civilizations. Throughout history, ancient societies applied the patterns found in nature to their philosophies, religions, and, subsequently, architecture and arts.

Although Letty's mind was troubled from a young age and influenced by her multiple personality disorder, she firmly believed in the power of geometric magic symbols for protection and healing. She was convinced that the full potential of sacred geometry was only known to the initiated, among whom she considered herself front and center. Letty believed that the strongest association between geometry, symbols, and sacred teachings originated from ancient Greece. This knowledge, she concluded, enabled Thales to predict the eclipse of the sun in 585 BC and formed the basis of the teachings of Pythagoras, as well as the symbolism in the artwork of Leonardo Da Vinci.

Or perhaps it is just the rewriting of historical events to suit.

Regardless of reality, Letty believed that human society did not seek the cause of these mathematically predictable natural events, preferring instead to attribute them to the inherent complexity of nature. It was nature's rhythmic frequency that caused the sun to rise, created earthquakes, and sometimes blotted out the sun. To Letty, it was the magic of patterns that allowed the prediction of these events with the permission of God, serving as a sign to the population and marking significant events. Not by any miracle, Letty predicted her own death on the fourth cycle of the solar eclipse to occur in 2023 that coincided with the appearance of the Leonard Commet trans-versing the near earth universe.

However, before the appearance of the Leonard Comet, Letty's fascination with patterns and prediction had grown into a consuming obsession. She delved into the arcane realms of low-frequency resonance signals, merging them with synthetic cognitive enhancements to plunge herself into deep, trance-like dream states. Over time and with meticulous practice, Letty unlocked an extraordinary ability to discern intricate patterns in human behaviour within these altered states. She could observe the lives of others, subtly influencing their actions and even becoming an active participant in their life trajectories.

To refine her skills, Letty engaged in a peculiar kind of target practice, selecting unsuspecting individuals as subjects for her experiments. This often had unintended and sometimes catastrophic consequences for those involved. The ethical lines blurred as her quest for understanding and control took precedence over the well-being of her targets.

Dream States

Central to Letty's experiences in these dream states were her alter personalities, Alan and Sarah. She believed that these alter egos were extensions of her own consciousness, intricately woven into the fabric of her mind. In these altered states, Alan and Sarah were not merely figments of her imagination; they were her companions and collaborators, her dream ego partners with whom she shared her life's journey.

However, this extraordinary capability came at a steep cost. Each time Letty immersed herself in the life patterns of Alan or Sarah, she left behind fragments of her own psyche. It felt as if someone was siphoning away her mind, never to be fully reclaimed. The toll on her mental state was profound, leading to an ever-growing sense of fragmentation and loss.

In these last days leading up to the comet's appearance, Letty's dream journeys grew increasingly perilous. The boundaries between her waking life and the dream states blurred, making it difficult for her to distinguish reality from the constructs of her mind. The more she ventured into the lives of Alan and Sarah, the more she struggled to maintain her own sense of self.

Yet, despite the risks, Letty pressed on, driven by an unshakeable belief in the importance of her work. She saw herself as a pioneer, exploring the uncharted territories of consciousness and human potential. To her, the sacrifices she made were justified by the profound insights she gained and the possibilities they opened for the future.

In her final, most daring experiment, Letty attempted to synchronize the patterns of her mind with the expected celestial patterns of the Leonard Comet. She believed that this alignment would unlock a new level of understanding, a fusion of cosmic and cognitive rhythms that would transcend her current limitations. But as the comet streaked across the sky, the strain on her mind reached its breaking point.

Letty's consciousness splintered, fragments of Alan and Sarah's lives merging with her own in an irreversible fusion. Afterward, Letty ended up in a liminal state where she was no longer fully herself, but a complex amalgamation of the personas she had so intimately intertwined with. Her innovative work, although providing incredible insights, had also pushed her to the brink of her own sanity, demonstrating the risks of delving too deeply into the mysteries of the mind.

A Beautiful Mind.

Letty found the volatile and damaged mind of Alan Irvenko attractive. She recognized he was explosively violent, with sociopathic tendencies that frightened everyone around him. But not Letty. She nurtured and cultured the young man as her own flesh and blood. In her mind, she kept him close by employing him. She watched him; his behavioral patterns fascinated the old woman. She felt the power of his youth again. A primordial feeling of pulsing muscles and a no-fear existence. This physical bruteness of Alan, his youthful energy, was exactly what Letty needed in her own life.

To some extent, this fascination with Alan made her drop her guard as she ventured her mind further and further into the darker recesses of this young man's consciousness. This untampered fascination, combined with reckless determination to extend her cognitive function, eventually cost Letty dearly. Letty had believed that she could nurture and ultimately control the damaged Alan and set about a plan to transfer a controlling part of her consciousness to his mind. She practiced concentrating on her brain, on her thoughts. She imagined the darkness within her head. A space occupied by a pulsing biological mass sealed inside a boney cave with no light in total silence.

The constant barrage of electrical pulses coming from our senses, the only connection to the outside world. The magic of how these electrical signals transform into the perception of the world as objects, people and places filled with color, shape and texture. This is our consciousness, creating a prediction of a perceived reality. Letty's fears of aging and how her brain was counting down to an end point she already knew surfaced and swirled around in her head. The empathic and sympathetic voice of Sarah cried and sobbed quietly in the darkness. The violent and angry voice of Alan laughed out loud and shouted to be heard.

Without her own bodily constraints or boundaries, the thoughts of a damaged and dangerous mind perplexed Letty. She believed she could fool aging and live on in the mind of the much younger host with the physical strength of youth that lives in the space between fight or flight.

Letty Stark self predicted her own death in 2023 and left behind a legacy of scientific research and experimentation in cognitive enhancement. At least in Letty's mind, she believed she could access her research post mortem through Alan's consciousness. This assumed, of course, that she could control the thoughts and mind of the younger Alan.

In the aftermath of Letty's passing, the professional business faced a public backlash and legal repercussions for the unethical practices that had taken place under Letty's guidance. The shadowy and secretive company owned by Letty was shut down, and the participants of the trials were left to deal with the aftermath of the experiments.

However, transferring Letty's consciousness into Alan Irvenko's mind was only partially successful, and the experiment had left Alan with severe mental maladies inherited from Letty that had only worsened with time. Alan now also suffered multiple personality disorder symptoms and heard the voices of others in his sleep. This not only included the voice of Letty, but also Letty's own mind created memories.

Regardless of the ethical and moral principles involved, Letty's mind believed she had still made significant contributions to the scientific community. Her research had led to breakthroughs in cognitive enhancement, and her experimentation with low frequency brain wave entrainment had opened up new possibilities for the understanding of the human mind.

Letty's fascination with patterns caused by extreme Apophenia (pattern identification) and people-watching had led her down a path that ultimately cost her own life. In the end, her thirst for knowledge and experimentation had consumed her, leaving behind a legacy to be remembered for both its contributions and its tragedies.

As for Alan Irvenko, he remained a shadowy figure, haunted by the memories and experiences of the past. His mind, damaged and volatile, remained in a fragile state; and the memories of Letty's experiments and manipulation continued to haunt him.

The legacy of Letty Stark is a complex and layered one, full of both triumphs and tragedies. Her life and work serve as a reminder of the boundless potential of the human mind, but also of the dangers that lie within. It is up to future generations to learn from her successes and failures, to continue to push the boundaries of what is possible, but also to be mindful of the risks and consequences that come with such pursuits.

GENETIC EVOLUTION

In the beginning, long before Letty Stark or mind laboratories existed, an ancient tribe gathered on a clifftop. The first of the mind travelers stared into the black night, seeing patterns in the stars. Each interpreting their own meaning from the constellations that seemed to peer back at the small group assembled. Slowly, as soon as the revelation was understood, each dropped their eyes and looked to the others. One of them spoke.

"We see what others cannot because we are chosen. No one hears or sees more than another. We are gifted to see the meanings that others choose not to see. The patterns in the stars, the movement of the tide and the master-plan of nature itself."

The speaker stepped to the edge of the precipice and, with his arm, swept a wide arc across the sky. He turned to his brethren and looked at each one. "Brothers. I hear your minds as you do mine."

What is it that defines who a person is? Is it personality, a combination of relatively fixed traits, or how we behave or look? Are we determined by our genetic makeup? A product of evolutionary genetics learned through patterns over hundreds of years.

Perhaps destiny determines who we are. That this moment, reading this book right now, is exactly who and where you are supposed to be.

Today, more than others, the multiple personalities of Letty Stark, Alan Irvenko and Sarah Ryan asked each other these questions in unison. Today, it resonated even louder as they heard the words delivered from the pulpit over the coffin and biological shell of their surrogate and mentor, Letty Stark. A eulogy written by Letty to signal to those left behind a message. At least, this was the interpretation of the impressionable Alan and Sarah.

Alan was not a religious man but fascinated by the ceremony of religion. Perhaps it was his inherited interest of sacred geometry from Letty. He watched intently as the young priest stepped down from his altar. Down the three or four steps of the plush red carpet to stand before the ornately decorated coffin covered in magic symbols of geometric patterns whose meaning is lost to modern science and the non-initiated. The priest swung an equally ornate orb in one hand while splashing its blessed contents with the other.

Alan wondered to himself; how young the priest was. A very red, boyish-looking face with those wispy side brows that suggested a boy who had not yet started shaving. Alan shrugged his shoulders as a chill crept over him. The church was cold. The octagonal-tiled floor pattern supporting the hard wooden pews for the worshippers. All hard surfaces, thought Alan, wondering if this was intentional to remind those on their knees to know their place. In contrast, the altar was raised and covered in a deep pile of carpet. The ceremonial priest's chair was ornate. It even had a color-matching cushion.

As the young boy priest swung his orb and chanted his verse, Alan's attention changed to the body of the old woman laid out in the open coffin. He recognized her, of course, as his old boss and matriarch, the one and only Letty Stark. Except Alan knew it was not her, really. It was simply the body of an old woman laid out in a wooden box, getting splashed by tap water from a priest who looked like he has yet to graduate to a shaving blade.

She looks well; he thought. Almost healthy. If that is even possible for a dead person. Undertaker makeup can do a lot nowadays and Letty looked twenty years younger. At least in the mind of Alan. Glancing around at the mourners, he realized he did not know many of them. Aside from the few business colleagues, and Letty's other surrogate Sarah, he recognized no one else. *No harm anyway*, he thought.

"Sorry for your loss," expressed the boy priest, now standing before Alan with his white, soft, powdered, perfumed hand extended.

Alan's attention came back into focus, and he shook the hand of the priest. Clammy and limp. *No strength*, he thought to himself privately.

"She was a noble character and lived to a great age. This is a loss to the entire community."

Although not exactly certain what the priest was talking about, Alan nodded his head in agreement, at the same time tightening his lips so that the bottom one spilled over the top. The priest moved on to his next patron of need and repeated his mantra of condolences and platitudes.

After a few moments, Alan saw an opportunity to exit from his pew and took it readily. He slid out from the polished wood bench into the aisle and made his way towards the open coffin. The old woman's hands were joined across her midriff as though supporting her age-sagged breasts with her forearms. Fingers intertwined with rosary beads laced through them. She looked peaceful; in a way that all dead people do.

A release for her perhaps, he thought.

After all, she was getting frail in her old age. Alan still felt a strange sense of sadness looking at the shell of the old woman. His mind registered the visual information and processed the scene like a computer hard drive. No emotion or sorrow. He dropped his head as a last mark of reverence and turned his heels on his polished patent shoes to leave the cold church.

Once outside, he fixed his overcoat against the cold and damp air and cough-endured his cigarette. Letty had always hated his smoking. Perhaps as a signal from the grave, crows exclaimed their collective disapproval in the background. The black color contrasting against the gray sky that darkened and lightened as it dispensed its load in showers of rain.

"Alan, are you heading back to the office?" called an approaching voice from behind.

It was the voice of Sarah Ryan that Alan recognized instantly. It annoyed Alan that she was much younger than him. Sarah had an intenseness about her combined with intelligence that made Alan slightly uneasy.

"We have a lot of business to discuss and decisions to make."

Alan raised his glove-free smoking hand to acknowledge the request and nodded in agreement. Alan's inherited eyes were a sharp crystal blue that made it appear like he was looking straight through you. The same as Letty's.

"Business has to continue," he muttered and turned to walk towards the waiting cars. Taking the last deep drag on his cigarette, Alan flicked the ember end away into the dampness before sliding into his car.

The office was not far, and perhaps it was time to get back to business. After all, it was Letty who had founded the company, and for sure she would not want to see business lose ground already made.

As Alan drove back to the office, his mind drifted back to Letty Stark's favourite story of the ancient tribe on the clifftop. He contemplated the spoken words. "*We see what others cannot because we are chosen.*" He wondered if there was any truth to that statement. Was he chosen to be where he was at that very moment? Was he meant to be a part of Letty's legacy? Was it fate that led him to this point in his life?

Alan pushed the thoughts to the back of his mind as he pulled into the parking lot of the office building. As he walked through the doors, he could feel the weight of responsibility settling on his shoulders like a warm-blooded creature wrapping itself around his neck. Letty had entrusted him with a mission to continue her work in mind enhancement, and it was up to him to keep it thriving.

The next few weeks were a blur of meetings, decisions, and negotiations. Alan worked tirelessly to keep the research afloat. He could feel the stress and pressure building within him, but he pushed on. He was determined to honour Letty's legacy and keep her research alive.

As the months passed, Alan realized the truth in the ancient tribal words read out at Letty's funeral. He saw things others didn't. Just like his surrogate mother before him, he noticed patterns in the market that his colleagues overlooked. He believed he had a vision for the company that no one else could see. He also heard the growing whispers of Letty somewhere in the back of his mind, getting louder and louder.

Under Alan's leadership, the company soared. He made risky decisions that paid off, and the business grew exponentially. He knew Letty was deep down, proud of him.

As Alan sat in his office one day, reflecting on the past year, he realized he had become a different person. He was no longer just a man going through the motions of life. He had a purpose. He had drive and a vision.

Alan decided it wasn't fate that led him to this point. It wasn't a predetermined destiny he had no control over. It was his own choices and actions that led him here. He had taken on the responsibility of the company, and he had worked tirelessly to make it succeed.

Alan smiled to himself as he looked out the window at the city below. In his mind, he heard Letty whisper to him that there would be challenges ahead, but he was ready for them. He had found his purpose, and he was determined to see it through.

RELIGIOUS SERVICE

"You can take away the flowers from the church and place them on the grave," said the priest in a thick Irish accent as he looked on.

"It is such a waste. Someone spent a lot of money on the flower arrangements she did not even see."

"Yes, for sure, but obviously they can afford it."

The small room at the back of the main church served as a sort of storage or gowning room for the priest and assistants. Extending from the main church, the floor tiles continued into the priest's quarters, behind the main altar. The only difference was that there was radiator heating available in the private quarters. On the wall, holy pictures, or to be more exact, religious-themed pictures of scenes of petition, or atonement, or a choppy sea scene with a young woman raising her hand to the sky. As though desperately calling out to the deaf but dark, thundery sky for help. The running theme appeared to be death and despondence with humanity and life.

Father Hansen de-gowned from his funeral ceremony attire and carefully laid out the smock on the polished wooden counter. His underneath day-clothes partially hid the fact that he was a priest in the church of somewhere, something, or somebody. The black trousers from the other half of a poorly fitted suit, and the out-of-a-packet white shirt offset with a neck chain and cross that an urban rapper would be proud to wear. The chain and cross, that is. It is doubtful that anyone except priests and undertakers would wear the pants and shirt.

"Shall I put away the holy orb, Father?" spoke a nun as she glided into the sacristy. "It was a lovely funeral ceremony today. Do you think she would have approved?"

"I think so. Although it was not so well-attended. Aside from Sarah, her stepdaughter, and the strange-looking Alan, I suppose she had no actual family left to speak of."

Sister Anne deftly folded the holy garments as she slipped them in a dust protector for the next holy event. She had probably done this folding exercise a million times and felt blessed every time she did.

"That young chap, Alan Irvenko, is certainly strange. Did you get to speak to him after?" asked the nun as she carefully washed her hands with water and the blessed soap.

Father Hansen fixed his collar, genuflected, and blessed himself before answering.

"Yes, I did afterwards–just briefly, though. Struck me as very distant, perhaps a bit detached. During our conversation, I thought he was looking straight through me."

Sister Anne joined her two hands under her chin and dropped her eyes to the floor before the superiority of the priest. She stood in anticipation. After a brief hesitation, Father Hansen acceded, making a sign of the cross in the air over her, and his lips spoke without a sound as though speaking in silence. The nun reciprocated and blessed herself before looking up as Father Hansen left for the evening.

The nun continued her routine clean-up jobs around

the small holy room, that included collecting up all the individual mass cards and remembrance notices placed on top of the coffin during the ceremony. Sister Anne had a macabre interest in opening and reading memorial cards. She thought it might be a sin but excused the behavior because it was an act of kindness to read the comment cards before placing them inside the coffin with the deceased. After all, if no one else was going to read them, she reflected to herself. Anyway, she confessed her sins every morning, and this absolved her from mortal sin.

As she opened each of the small white envelopes with generic images of white flowers or scenes of a castle on a hill, she came across one that stood out. It was not the usual standard card of condolences. She opened the card and read the words.

Dear Letty,

Sincere congratulations on your prompt departure.
Although your body is gone, your mind and wishes will live on through your emissaries.
Death calls only to those that want to hear.
Alan & Sarah.

The pious nun pondered the meaning and kept the card as a private memento to add to her slightly macabre collection of sympathy cards. She carefully returned the card to its white envelope and placed it in her gown pocket. The rest of the cards she collected and placed inside a small pouch bag and returned to the coffin, to place the pouch bag inside with the departed soul before final internment.

Before leaving the church that evening, Sister Anne checked that the church was locked up, and all was as it should be. The loneliness of the casket at the top of the church, ready for its last journey in the morning, gave an eerie feeling as the light switches were turned off row by row. The click of each light row echoed in the open space. The religious woman felt strange. Although she had done this routine many times, she felt an unfamiliar presence that evening. As though someone was watching her.

As Sister Anne walked through the empty darkened church, she couldn't shake off the feeling of unease. She tried to brush it off as her imagination ran wild, but the hairs on the back of her neck stood up. She turned around, but no one was there. The Nun continued to walk towards the exit, but she couldn't shake off the feeling of being followed.

As she reached the door, she heard a faint sound. It was coming from the altar. She slowly made her way towards the altar, her heart beating faster with each step. When she reached the altar, she saw a figure standing there.

It was Alan Irvenko.

"What are you doing here?" Sister Anne asked, surprised.

"I had to come back," Alan replied, his voice barely above a whisper.

Sister Anne could see the pain in his eyes, and she knew he needed someone to talk to. She motioned with urgency for him to follow her to the sacristy, and they sat down.

Alan opened up about his relationship with Letty. He told Sister Anne how she had become a surrogate mother to him and Sarah and had grown close. He also revealed that Letty had confided in him about her wishes to end her life on her own terms on an exact date and time to coincide with a solar eclipse. Alan still did not understand how it was that her body was deceased, but he could still feel her presence.

Sister Anne listened intently, trying to provide comfort and understanding. As Alan spoke, she remembered the card he had left for Letty. Incriminating herself, she pulled it out of her pocket and showed it to him.

"What does this mean?" she asked.

Alan looked at the card and sighed. "It was our little secret.

Letty and I had talked about it. It was her way of telling me she was ready to die."

Sister Anne was shocked. She couldn't believe what she was hearing. But as she looked at Alan, she could see the pain and grief in his eyes.

"I don't know what to do," Alan said, his voice cracking.

Sister Anne placed a hand on his shoulder. "I'll pray for you," she whispered. As they sat in silence, Sister Anne realized that there was more to Letty's story than she had initially thought. She felt a sense of compassion and empathy towards Alan and Letty. They had made a hard choice, and she knew she couldn't judge them for it.

As Alan left, Sister Anne remained in the sacristy, deep in thought. She thought about Letty, Alan, and the choices they had made. She thought about the fragility of life and how we all must face our mortality one day.

As she looked up at the religious-themed pictures on the wall, she felt a sense of peace wash over her. She knew that her role as a nun was to provide comfort and support to those in need without judgement. She prayed for Letty, for Alan, and for all those who were struggling with the pain of loss and grief.

In the end, Sister Anne realized that life is precious, and we must cherish every moment we have with those we love. She knew Letty had made a choice, but she hoped that she had found peace in the end.

As she left the church, Sister Anne looked back at the casket one last time. She said a silent prayer for Letty, and for all those who had passed on. And as she walked away, she knew she would always carry a piece of Letty's story with her.

◆ ◆ ◆

LIFE IS BUSINESS

L ike every other day, Alan Irvenko pulled up to his assigned parking space at the front of the office. Stepping out of his car, he stared for a moment at the façade of a glass building in front of him. An impressive office building, he thought. It has worn well over the years. The towers of dark gray steel and glass stretched up towards the sky, broken only by the large block signage that read "Mind Keeper Inc."

The local lad has done well for himself, he thought, as he stepped out of the car. He breathed in deeply and made the short walk to the security entrance. The guard tipped his cap and formally greeted Alan.

"Good afternoon, Mr. Irvenko."

Alan did not answer and simply pushed through the secondary inner door that brought him into the cavernous reception area. Made of glass and exposed structural steel beams, the expanse of the area, the sheer vastness, intended to make visitors feel small. The receptionist, a young man, was busy talking on two phones. One phone in hand and another clamped between his collarbone and cheekbone. His free hand tapped a screen keyboard in front of him. Alan paid him no heed and breezed past to the elevators leading to the upper floors.

The glass-walled offices were impressive and gave the feel of openness and light in what was externally a dark grey skyline that stretched across the surrounding business district.

The boardroom was already occupied as he entered the suit-filled room of colleagues talking amongst themselves in a low tone. Alan took his seat, that their departed founder and CEO, Letty Stark had previously occupied.

"Good morning, ladies and gentlemen," he addressed them as he adjusted his seat. "Apologies for the slight delay in starting the meeting. Shall we begin please with the first item?"

The table bustled for a minute as people shuffled papers and pens clicked, ready to scribe. The projector screen buzzed to life, and the first PowerPoint title came into focus.

"Clinical Trial Mind Sight No 001A," by Dr. Sarah Ryan Ph.D.

Before standing, Dr. Ryan rubbed the palms of her hands nervously on her navy skirted thighs. She stood abruptly while reaching to stretch the bottom of her skirt awkwardly to get as close to covering her knees as possible. She swung her chair sideways and stepped out from the long table, stepping forward to the side of the projector screen to face her audience. As her surrogate mother before her, Sarah Ryan was the picture of beautiful, controlled confidence and could command the room.

She clicked a remote-control device and the presentation deck advanced.

In Presentation Mode

"The aim of the Mind Sight trial is to show a reduction in aggressive responses through electrical stimulation of the amygdala section of the brain, ultimately improving on stress responses in patients suffering a predisposition to anxiety and volatile behavior. Participants in the trial showed a minimal response in a before and after case study and results are inconclusive at this midpoint review."

She clicked on her remote control again, while simultaneously turning to look at the display screen, before scanning the faces of her audience. Alan pushed his desk chair back, interlocking his two hands under his chin and narrowing his eyes, as though focusing on the information charts on the screen.

"What behavioral changes were noticed, if any?" he asked in a clear voice from the back of the room.

"The Emotional Intelligence test results show minimal change when compared against the control group, but there is a statistically significant improvement in self-awareness markers for individuals in the test group that may be related to an improved stress response."

As though awaiting an acknowledgement, Dr. Ryan paused at this point and looked down at the long table at Alan.

"That's not what I asked."

Dr. Ryan hesitated for a moment to think before she continued.

"Well, interestingly, thirteen of the fifteen showed reduced rational thought capacity and electrical activity in the frontal lobes while there was high signal activity in the emotional centers of the brain. This suggests that behavioral volatility is an emotional response that an external signal influence may precipitate."

One delegate at the table raised an index finger to signal a question. Dr. Ryan was glad to take the intense scrutiny from her momentarily and at once ceded to the request.

"Please go ahead," she nodded towards the delegate.

"Sarah, are you saying that inhibition of the frontal lobe area results in increasingly volatile behavior responses, including uncontrolled aggression?"

"Yes. Based on the preliminary data and a low trial population size, but essentially that assertion is correct."

Alan rubbed his left shoulder hard and reached to the back of his neck, as though trying to scratch. He kept his gaze on the screen.

"Can we control or suppress participant aggression through stimulation of activity in the frontal lobe?" asked Alan. This time without raising a finger.

He momentarily turned his gaze to his laptop screen, as though pondering the thought, before turning back to the presenter.

"And please answer the question as I have asked?"

"Subject to the limitation I have outlined, that is a reasonable assumption to make from the data. However, I want to be clear. We are talking about uncontrolled rage response by individuals that could, in theory, result in unpredictable responses including violence."

Alan made a breathing noise like a large bull in a field as he inhaled and exhaled deeply through his nose. His brain clicked through the information he had just read and heard.

"Ok, let us leave it there for the moment. I would like an outline proposal by the end of the week to expand the trial program, including a more aggressive participant enrollment timeline. Thank you."

Alan abruptly ended the meeting and left the boardroom, leaving the others to reflect on what had happened and brainstorm ways to meet their new boss's expectations.

As Alan made his way back to his office, he couldn't help but feel a sense of unease. The results of the clinical trial were concerning, to say the least. While he had always been a firm

56

believer in the potential of neuroscience, that Mind Sight *might* make people more volatile was deeply troubling. He wondered if this was why Letty had become more and more distant with him in the months preceding her demise.

He took a seat at his desk and opened his laptop, scrolling through the presentation slides once more. As he did so, he realized the data was inconclusive at best, and yet he had already expanded the trial program at the Sun Care Residential Home for the aging.

With doubt coursing through his frontal synapses, he wondered if perhaps he had been too hasty in his decision-making. After all, the potential risks and consequences outweighed the benefits. He needed to think this through more carefully.

Just then, his phone rang, interrupting his thoughts. In the earpiece, he heard the voice he recognized of his surrogate sibling. It was Sarah Ryan.

"Hey, Sarah," he said breezily, picking up the phone without hesitation.

"Alan, following up from the meeting earlier, I was concerned that you cut it short. How did it go afterwards?"

"Well," he paused as he thought. "We discussed the clinical trial results for Mind Vault. I know they were inconclusive, but I've decided to expand the program. Imagine if we could harvest consciousness and store into a digital bank for future study and research. We are close Sarah. I can feel it."

There was a long pause on the other end of the line before Sarah spoke again.

"Alan, I'm concerned. If the results are inconclusive, shouldn't we wait until we have more data before we make strategic research direction decisions?"

Alan sighed almost apologetically into the phone. He knew she was right but was frustrated by her lack of enthusiasm for his mind harvesting storage idea.

"You're right, Sarah. I think I may have jumped the gun on this one. The pattern is not identified. I need to take a step back and re-evaluate the situation."

"That's a wise choice," Sarah replied. "Remember, we're dealing with people's lives and Letty's lifelong work. We need to be careful."

Alan hung up the phone, feeling sarcastically grateful for the words of wisdom from an empath such as Sarah. He realized he needed to approach this situation more carefully, with the potential consequences in mind.

Over the next few days, he worked closely with the research team to review the data from the clinical trial. They conducted further tests and experiments on the elderly residents of the Care Home to determine the potential risks and benefits of the Mind Sight program. The ultimate aim was to prolong human life by the transferring of aging, but healthy minds, into physically younger hosts. In order to achieve this goal, a solution to harvest and store an individual's consciousness was a critical step.

Ultimately, Alan knew inside that stopping the trail works could not happen. The risks were high, but so also were the potential benefits. In the long term, humanity could benefit from the revolutionary concept of transferring the consciousness from deceased hosts to a digital storage system. The ability for future generations to mind store their consciousness to ensure extended longevity and an end to dementia and brain disease. *Who, in their right minds, would not want this?* He thought to himself.

Somewhere deep in the recess of his own mind, he thought he could hear the clapping and cheering of Letty Stark.

As he looked out at the impressive glass building that housed Mind Keeper's research laboratories, he felt proud of what they had accomplished, but also aware of the responsibility that came with his position. He knew he had a duty to the company and its employees, but also to the broader community and, of course, the living consciousness of Letty Stark. And she insisted on reminding him of this duty regularly.

Alan was determined to fulfil that duty with care and consideration, always keeping in mind the potential impact of his actions.

CONSCIOUS TRANSFER: PROTOTYPE 01

"**J**ust try to relax, Letty. Your mind is adjusting, that's all, and needs more time." Deep brown eyes flickered and stared back with confusion. Tired with age, her eyes also showed fear. Perhaps knowing death was near, or perhaps the uncertainty of what comes next.

"You're going to be fine. You are connected to the MRI, and everything looks good," announced the lab technician, fussing around the bed.

Letty's eyes closed against the sharpness of the bright laboratory lighting, and she felt the warm infusion of a drug cocktail into her arm take hold. Unable to discern the passing of time, she first sensed a change in temperature. It was markedly colder.

Letty opened her eyes slowly to the darkness. She tried to

focus her eyes, but there was nothing but blackness within the confined space of her head. There was no sound, no light, just an empty darkness that fully enveloped her. An unfamiliar scent of burned incense lingered that filled her nostrils. She could feel her body, her legs stretched out as far as they could. Her arms across her chest. She suddenly heard a voice. Distant at first, and not coherent. It grew louder, as though someone had just opened the door on the black space.

"Okay, okay, you are fine now. Can you hear me, Letty? Time to wake up now."

Her eyes blinked, and her pupils dilated with the bright light of exposure. She felt a rush of air fill her lungs that she took gladly. Her eyes watered with a sense of relief.

The attending medics removed tubes and wires and disconnected the various medical monitors. Switches turned off loudly, and footsteps came and went.

"Can you squeeze my hand for me please, Letty dear?" asked the attendant in a slightly condescending voice as she took hold of her patient's hand and leaned in closer.

The attendant felt the sudden grip of her hand tighten tenfold and twist.

Letty pulled the attendant nearer. "Don't call me fucking 'Letty' again," came the voice from her mouth, almost involuntarily. It was as if her thoughts and voice were separate and independent of each other.

The handgrip tightened and pulled the nurse's face closer, so that she felt the full wrath in the voice and the powerful, almost overwhelming odor of stale tobacco. It was an unexpected strength from an aging old woman and felt like the strength of a youthful man. Another medic intervened and grabbed the nurse attendant across the shoulders, pulling her away. The grip released, and the nurse recoiled back from the bed. She gathered herself and was visibly shaken, accepting comfort from her colleagues.

Laying in the bed was the physical presence of Letty Stark, merged with the strength of Alan Irvenko. Her face raged with anger, as though a thunderous storm was ready to release a lightning bolt. Her clenched fists restricted blood flow, and the back of her hands were white. A male physician approached the bedside.

"Letty, are you ok? Do you know where you are?"

Letty blinked her eyes more than needed, shaking her head like a wild horse before breathing deeply as she finally looked to the ceiling.

"Yes, I'm fine. I think."

"And do you know where you are?"

"We are at the Mind Keeper's research clinic for mind harvesting," responded Letty.

Several attendant medics now gathered around the bedside of their chief executive officer and the signatory on their paychecks.

"Can you describe the experience?" ventured one of the attending doctors.

Letty nodded agreement and pulled herself upright, supported by the pillows behind her.

"It was not like before. I had no control over the host. In this dream, I could not even open my eyes to see anything. And at one point, I felt as if something heavy was holding me down."

The medics looked at each other and exchanged comments before returning to their subject.

"So, you were in a coma dream state for six hours and you can recall nothing in that time frame that would show conscious presence or any visual details?"

"No, it felt like minutes. I had a sense that I was somewhere else, someone else. It felt like a church, and I was speaking to a stupid Catholic Nun," rasped the old woman from her bed.

"I was completely incapacitated and not able to move. You must have gotten the resonate frequency wrong or perhaps given the incorrect dosage."

"I can assure you, Letty, that we do not make such mistakes."

"Just do your jobs. You are not paid to make mistakes," growled Letty back uncharacteristically. She then unceremoniously dismissed the medics with a wave of her hand.

Outside in the corridor, several of the doctors reflected on the day's events

"We are taking this too far. The old woman's brain is confused with the mind and thoughts of the psychotic Irvenko and showing signs of rejection. We were in unchartered territory before, but now we are heading into orbit."

"I agree. She is showing more volatility than expected and showing signs of psychopathic tendency. I fear we may be heading for the dark side and cannot control the mood shift."

Almost at the same time, the medics turned to look back through the wire mesh infused glass window at their subject. Now fully dressed in her dark business suit and white shirt, Letty stared back in disdain for them through the window. She stared harder, not moving. Transfixed on the faces of those staring back at her, as though reading, or interpreting, their thoughts.

The medics felt uneasy, as though under watch. They quickly dispersed like sheep who had sensed the nearby presence of a wild dog.

In the next room. Alan Irvenko lay in the medical bed stirring as if from a deep sleep. Compared to the patient next door, he had fewer white coats around him, but holding a firm grip on his hand was Dr. Sarah Ryan.

"Alan, are you awake"? asked Sarah in a caring tone.

Alan nodded his head slightly and a warm smile went across

his face that Sarah recognized. Both surrogate siblings' eyes welled up as their emotion centers fired.

Later that evening, Alan returned home to his apartment complex alone. He was quieter than usual, not speaking to anyone since leaving the clinic some hours ago. He stood at the stainless-steel lift doors, looking up to see the floor number count upwards, one after the other. Each of the neon orange numbers lit up as the sequence counted. Now and then, the lift's journey interrupted as someone got on or got off.

Even a lift floor counting from the ground to the top appeared as a pattern to be predicted. Alan's internal prediction machine considered the time of evening, the total number of building occupants, approximate age profile, and the total number of floors from top to ground. He estimated that after a fifteen-floor ascent, with four stops in the lower ten floors, that on reaching the penthouse floor, the lift should have an occupancy number of one person with a certainty factor of zero-point-seven.

A chime announced the lift arrival on the desired floor as the shiny steel doors opened. Alan stepped back to enable its passenger to step out first. A tall, smart-dressed woman stepped out from the interior and momentarily glanced at Alan before turning away again. Alan's gaze followed her for longer than necessary. He recognized her as someone he had met before, but could not retrieve the name from memory.

Alan placed a hand to hold the lift doors open before finally making the rest of the journey to his floor.

As Alan entered his apartment, he pulled the knot of his blue tie to loosen and dropped his briefcase to the floor before flopping backwards on to the bed. For seconds that felt like minutes, he stared at the ceiling above him, looking for minor imperfections in the ceiling plaster that might give him an answer to some totally unrelated question. He wondered if there is a mathematical equation or pattern of numbers that could predict the small dimples of dried paint where the painter had perhaps held the brush too long over a single point on the ceiling or had just lazily dipped the brush into the white emulsion paint for 2 seconds longer than he should have. His mind thoughts rolled as though tumbling down the side of a steep grassy embankment.

Each thought turning over and over. Sunlight, darkness, wetness and dry, warm, and cold. In addition, number patterns ran through his head, and he started calling out loud the Fibonacci number sequence to slow his stumbling mind thoughts. Eventually, the tumble slowed and his mind calmed to the moment that enabled him to stop his count mantra.

With his eyes still closed and arms and legs splayed across the bedcover, he suddenly noticed another presence. He held his eyes closed and breathed deeply, aware of the presence but not yet willing to engage. There was something familiar about this feeling that, on one hand, comforted Alan, and yet presented as a danger. Alan breathed deeply through his nostrils that flared and made a noise on the intake.

Then a soft voice inside his mind spoke to him.

Not threatening. Just a soft whisper voice that was not yet discernible. It was the voice of a female.

Alan... Alan, do you hear me yet?

Alan zoned in on the internal voice, feeling the familiar tone as it came into focus. In the next second, Alan realised it was the voice of his surrogate mother, Letty Stark. This time his eyes popped open, and he stared intently upwards, waiting for the next sound.

ALAN.... Came the voice louder and clearer this time.

Alan sat up quickly on the bed with confusion across his face. He turned his head slowly to look on either side of him in the partially darkened room, offset only by moonlight streaking through the cracks in the curtains.

I am still with you Alan; the test was a success. I feel your physical strength and presence as though mine. I sense your rage, my child— fear not, for I am with your consciousness as one.

Alan paused. He heard the words but was not sure if this was his imagination or was it the inconceivable alternative that he was hearing the voice of someone who had died. Someone who had transferred a conscious mind from her own and into his mind.

"Letty—is it really you"? asked Alan, although not sure he wanted to know the answer.

I am with you in consciousness, Alan. I feel you. Can you feel me? Came back the voice of Letty Stark's conscious mind.

ANGER RELEASE

Back at the clinic, the research support team reviewed the fMRI printouts of brain scans associated with the mind transfer trial protocol Letty-S 021. The conversations were initially jumbled as each of the researchers talked over the other and leaned across the charts, pointing at some spike that supported a particular hypothesis.

"I think we must get real here, folks. This is going to be a problem," exclaimed one associate, urgently pointing his finger at the wall chart.

"Look, we can't reverse the process now. It's already done. We have no choice."

This louder tone had the desired effect and brought the room to silence as each of the associates looked up and eventually took a seat. Their facial expressions looked resigned to the inevitability of an outcome that was now beyond their control.

"So, who is going to tell Mr. Irvenko?" asked one of the junior associates, a certain amount of nervousness in her tone.

"Clearly, we cannot continue this experiment. It is completely out of control."

"But there is no choice. We must continue. We cannot stop the irreversible sequence of events that are already in play. The brain signal, the consciousness of Letty Stark, is firmly ingrained in the brain of the new host. The best hope now is that the sequence will run itself out and stop before the situation becomes totally untenable. What is the worst-case scenario?"

Each of the associates looked around at each other as they thought about the question and the consequences that the answer will bring. A junior associate got to her feet and walked to the display board. She took a printed brain scan chart out and blue-tacked it onto the display board.

"This scan illustrates beta plaque deposits deep throughout the hippocampus region, resulting in inhibition of the neural pathways to respond to emotional stimuli. We have all seen this before in patients presenting with various psychosis. Simply put, this individual will not have constraints of emotions on their behaviors and will act out impulses with no thought on consequences."

One of the research associates raised his index finger to signal a question. Hesitantly.

"Perhaps we should pull the plug on the next batch of brain trials?"

If thoughts could be heard, the room would have filled with the sound of a symphony playing at full crescendo.

Back at the apartment, Alan Irvenko was sitting on the side of his bed, looking at his watch, completely unaware that he was the subject of a heated conversation across town. His eyes followed the stepping sweep of the clock's second hand as it followed its predetermined path. How simplistic, yet with hidden complexity, that made the wonder of timekeeping seem such a mundane task. In between seconds, invisible to the human eye, the watch mechanism turned and retained its timekeeping. For a moment, he considered why human eyes cannot see the movement between one second and the next. What exactly happens in milliseconds that we cannot see?

The darkness closed in around him as he lay back on his linen sheets. Alan moved the palms of his hands slowly across the sheets as though checking the material. Like an angel flexing its wings, he brought his arms from his side out to the edge of the bed and slowly back to his side. He fought sleep for as long as he could before finally drifting away, not knowing what dreams awaited his confused mind.

Alan's brain infused with the consciousness of the analytical Letty Stark. The contrasting minds fought each other for existence. Like some uninvited guest, the thoughts in his mind churned with conflict, dancing around the thoughts of Letty Stark. In his dreams, he saw faces of people he did not know, recalled memories of places he had never been, and heard voices of people he had never heard before. His brain tried relentlessly to reconcile the thoughts that flew through his mind like a murmuration of starlings in a clear evening sky. Twisting, turning in unison, as the black ghost darted across a sky of haze blue.

Alan's conscious mind came to the fore as though wrestling to take back control of the brain, its thoughts, and emotions. Like a hero breaking ranks, stepping forward to organize the chaos when no one else will. He got to his feet and threw a coat over his shoulders, heading out into the night.

Alan's mind took him to an unfamiliar dark street. It was late, and the streets were empty, except for the stray cat that slowly crossed the empty road at its leisure. Not knowing why he was here or even where exactly he was, his senses were overloaded as they fed information back to a confused mind.

As if from a cliché movie scene, the ground was black wet, as though just after a rain shower, and the overhead electricity lines glistened with beads of sweat.

Alan pulled the handle of a door leading to a brightly lit hallway and entered the small local bar. After the bright lights of the entrance hallway, the bar was gloomy and dark, as though to provide a level of anonymity to its patrons. There were only a few patrons, and Alan took a seat at the bar. Without asking, as though knowing it already, the bartender placed a short tumbler drink on the counter and then turned away while wiping his hands on a dirty tea cloth. The hands looked rough, with tufts of hair sprouting from knuckles and the dry skin effect of excessive exposure to washing up liquid. Or perhaps eczema.

A youngish, eye pleasing woman sat down, taking the stool beside Alan. She pulled the wooden stool out from under the counter almost clumsily and swung her shape onto the hard seat. Without speaking, she acknowledged the bartender with the deftest nod of her head and pout of her lips. The glisten of an overly pink lipstick was striking and enticing at the same time. Her lips appeared to glisten in the gloomy light of the bar.

As if unable to resist, like animal instincts, his senses absorbed the perfumed aroma of the woman next to him. Alan turned his head slowly to notice the woman and take in her presence.

Initially, she ignored Alan as she exercised her long neck. Slowly moving her head from one side to the other, rolling her neck on her shoulders. Alan could not help notice the whiteness of the skin on her neck area not touched by makeup or exposed to sunlight. The slight blueness of the veins in the neck was not overly prominent, but just a detail of attention that only someone like Alan would notice.

She slowly, and intentionally, stroked her stretched throat that made her neck look even longer. With one hand, she pushed her long blonde hair back from her face and deftly flicked it over her shoulder. Alan felt his mind go into free fall.

In a tight black pencil skirt that restricted movement, the woman purposely crossed her legs, one over the other, slowly, as she turned to look at Alan.

For a few moments, she just stared at him. Her eyes were a crystal blue that looked like a glass tumbler of ice. She made an expression with her mouth as she pursed her lips tightly. Her skin was like clingfilm, sucking in the face around the already prominent cheekbones and jawline. She leaned forward towards Alan. Ever so slightly to bring her eye line below Alan's and just enough so he could detect her scent. Alan was confused. He knew from his surrogate mother that the sense of scent was dormant during sleep and dream states. Yet, here, in what he thought must be a dream, he could smell this woman next to him.

Alan knew that the brain cannot tell the difference between actual events and dreams. Although he was in a sleep state and dreaming, Alan's subconscious mind heard, saw, and felt the emotions of the scene so vividly. The interaction felt real, even if he was asleep in his apartment. His body temperature increased, reacting to the interaction, and a perspiration response engaged to counteract the emotionally driven temperature rise. Alan felt a bead of sweat rise on his forehead and run down the side of his face. The hypothalamic gland released hormonal signals as a basic evolutionary response to stimulation. Primitive survival instincts fired across the neuronal pathways in his mind that superimposed on his conscious thought patterns.

"Do I know you?" asked Alan coyly as he moved his head back to break the uncomfortable space between them.

His posture relaxed. He rested his elbow on the bar while holding the tumbler glass in his hand. His other hand resting on his upper thigh.

The woman responded to Alan's question by withdrawing away slightly. She pulled her neck back and lifted her head to a tall position. She turned her gaze to look at the back wall of the bar, as though counting the bottles stacked on the shelves over the bar counter.

Alan looked at her from a side view. The woman appeared to be muttering something to herself. Her lips were moving slightly, but Alan could not hear what she was saying.

This time, Alan leaned forward, bringing his shoulders in towards his chest into a submissive position. Looking up to her eyes, he tilted his head to one side, almost apologetic to signal the engagement.

"Have we met before?"
Turning her head quickly, she cast her eyes to meet Alan's.
"You don't remember?"

Alan moved back and took a longer look. The pause enabled his memory centers to process the image from the visual cortex against previously stored images in the short and long-term memory centers.

Eventually, his mind just lied. Or perhaps it simply timed out on the effort of recalling a memory.

"Why yes, I seem to vaguely remember you but can't put a finger on a name," he stuttered out unconvincingly in a plastic accent that was unnecessary.

"You have a look of someone who I might have met previously and whose name I should remember but can't right now?"

Alan paused without finishing the sentence. Realizing what he was saying made no sense to anyone outside of his own mind.

Alan's demeanor did not change with the discovery that he was sitting beside a woman, whom he remembered vaguely from somewhere in his distant memory, but uncertain of where. He was not disturbed or shocked. He felt no emotions or feelings either way. He had no remorse or regret, and instead turned his attention to the display of bottles that lined the back wall of the bar.

Like a meditation exercise, or perhaps a distraction technique, to offset discomfort, Alan counted the columns of bottles behind the bar on the wall display. His mind processed the calculation with ease, and he took comfort from his intelligence.

Staring at the wall of bottles, Phillip looked until he saw a pattern in the bottle display that teased his mind. He smiled slightly from the corner of his mouth as he took meaning from the simple calculations that told Alan that this was nothing more than his imagination, or a dream.

With this reality realization dawning on him, and as if to confirm his thoughts, a sudden but familiar sharp shock of pain raced up Alan's arm, through to his shoulder and finished behind his left ear. This caused an involuntary jerk that caused Alan to wince as the nerves spasmed in response. The bar scene faded in and out of focus until finally replaced with a white ceiling and walls of beige that was Alan's apartment.

Alan turned over in his bed onto his side. Placing both his hands between collar and his jaw, he curled up into a fetal position. It was a comfortable position. Something that drew him back to childhood, perhaps.

As Alan slept, his dreams were plagued with the memories and thoughts not of his own but of Letty Stark.

His brain, infused with the consciousness of another person, struggled to reconcile the conflicting thoughts and emotions that were not his own. In his dreams, Alan found himself in unfamiliar surroundings. His mind drifted readily from a dark street alone to a busy convenience store, to a conversation with a stranger.

Despite the apparent reality of the memories and dreams, Alan knew that this was not his life, that the memories and experiences that he was experiencing were not his own. He was an unwilling host, trapped in a body that was his own and a mind that was not, unable to control the thoughts and emotions that were flooding his mind.

Meanwhile, at the clinic, the research support team was reviewing the fMRI printouts of brain scans associated with brain trial B 021. They were urgently discussing the implications of their findings and the need to inform Alan Irvenko, the willing subject of the experiment.

The team had discovered that the brain signal and consciousness of Letty Stark was now firmly entrained in the brain of the new host body, and that the sequence of events set in motion could not be reversed. The worst-case scenario, they feared, was that the new host could act out impulses with no thought of the consequences, with no constraints of emotions on behaviour.

The researchers were torn between their sense of responsibility for what had happened and their inability to control the situation. They knew they could not stop the sequence of events that was already in play, but they were also aware of the potential dangers of continuing the experiment.

As Alan slept, his brain was struggling to make sense of the conflicting memories and emotions that were flooding his mind. He knew he was not the person he appeared to be, that his thoughts and experiences were not his own. He tried to fight the dreams, to resist the pull of the memories and emotions that were not his own, but it was a losing battle.

In the end, the worst-case scenario that the researchers had feared came to pass. Alan could not control the impulses and emotions that were flooding his mind, and acted out in ways that he could never have imagined. He caused harm to those around him, and there was a genuine fear that he could not be stopped, with ultimate death and misery on the horizon.

MORE TIME

Science has brought many advances in the last ten years that we mostly take for granted. Through technology, we can see microscopic life forms that previously we did not know existed. We can see far into the sky, to see distant galaxies, probe the nucleus of an atom, and measure the distance between far-off stars that have long since become extinct. But we cannot go there. We can learn about ancient civilizations through relics and excavated fossils, but we cannot go there either.

As a society, we look to the future and try to predict outcomes of decisions that are already made, climate change effects, weather predictions, the future of our species. We will get to the future soon enough. The only certainty is that we will wish for more time.

The consultant neurologists that examined the brain scans of Alan Irvenko realized with some comfort that Alan / Letty had little time left in this world. The aging brain that caused the separation of left and right brain hemispheres, a natural occurrence in healthy aging, appeared to be progressing faster than originally expected. Essentially, Alan was a young, capable man of thirty-five, with the aging brain of an eighty-three-year-old woman sharing his head. The normal maladies of healthy aging applied. Dementia, short-term memory loss, and a deterioration in emotional responses to stimuli. This made Alan Irvenko emotionally cold and without remorse. Essentially, without morality or ethical compass. Alan Irvenko could no longer tell the difference between right and wrong.

Later that morning, Alan arrived at the offices of Mind Keepers and parked in his usual space. He strolled across the car park through reception as though in a rush to get to his desk.

This was not unusual; he performed this routine every other morning. He followed his normal pattern as he time-checked the lift from floor fifteen to the lobby. Some days, he would complain to the utilities technicians that the lift travel time was slowing by fifteen seconds per day, and perhaps preventative maintenance was required within the next three weeks. However, people had become used to this behavior and expected nothing less from Mr. Irvenko.

His office colleagues were less tolerant of Mr. Irvenko's criticism and nuances for details that seemed irrelevant and sometimes, well, just rude. He would think nothing of pointing out personal nuances that crossed a professional boundary. Weight gains on others, opinions on wardrobe or hair, and seemed to be completely obsessed with the operating principles of the office photocopier. Flash, Print, Flash, Print, Load, Flash, Print, repeating over and over on its predetermined pattern of operation. He complained about everything as though an old age pensioner.

Alan had become an internal joke amongst the research scientists. The interns regularly joked with each other that Alan Irvenko's initial's A.I. was not a coincidence and that he was the original artificial intelligence. "Ask A.I. anything" they dared each other from the safe confines of the externally located smoking shelter. Of course, no one was brave enough to take the challenge.

The first meeting that morning, called by Alan, was with the Section Heads of the group. The business had become diversified under the previous CEO and included controlling interest in the many diversified interests of the business.

Although each of the business units were separate entities, there were overlapping dependencies that were leveraged. Mind Keepers required somewhat healthy mind volunteers for clinical trials. Next door, Sun Care Retirement Home had an aging and willing customer base eager to become involved in clinical trials. This suited the needs of Mind Keeper's research, demand for donors promised the ungodly specter of life ever after. This relationship served Letty and Alan's interests well in the past and he had plans to further develop, and leverage, this unique resource.

The Section Heads comprised a competent group of professionals with proven academic records. Diversified personality types that reflected the diversified nature of their own business units. They did not really like that; they answered to Alan Irvenko. He was perceived as under qualified, acutely detail-orientated, and erratic. Unpredictable. He expected answers that fitted with his own needs or expectations and could be demanding.

The morning meeting involved a roundtable of detailed updates from each business unit while Alan sat at the top of the table, taking notes. Like every other meeting, question-and-answer sessions that were daunting followed each update and felt like an interrogation by the CEO, who could challenge the smallest of details with the finesse of a Rottweiler who had just dug up its favorite bone.

The Section Head for Mind Keeper laboratories was also the only female board member. Sarah Ryan was a semi-competent business unit manager and, although not long in the role, she was considered a top performer with prospects within the organization. Before Letty Stark's passing, Letty mentored and groomed Sarah for the role, which earned Sarah a certain level of respect from her peers.

"Last quarter results are up on the previous quarter, with twelve cases successfully executed and a revenue generation of plus twenty percent," she reported with confidence. "Opportunities for growth are good, and we are looking to increase business in the next quarter by ten percent, reflecting a robust growth in our service market."

"What are the growth drivers?" asked Alan from his top table seat.

"One hundred percent of growth is coming through referrals from the nursing home. Age Care costs continue to rise. This is primarily driven by economic situations, market rising debt, employment challenges, and a high interest mortgage banking sector. The latter is responsible for a third of the growth projections."

Sarah Ryan paused at this point. She was a confident speaker and looked towards her new boss in anticipation of Alan's next question. And after a brief pause, it finally came.

"What are the perceived challenges to the business in the coming quarter?"

"Most of the challenges relate to ongoing inquiries into outstanding cases. Local police are still investigating the sudden unexplained death of a care home assistant by one of our patients, and this has created a slowdown in new case administration as we have updated procedures and policy since this case."

This perked the attention of Alan and other board members, who recognized the case reference and recalled that it was Alan who was the direct Project Manager at the time dealing with the case.

Alan looked to be thinking. Staring blankly, he recalled his dream from the previous night where he had a brief conversation at a bar with an attractive, seductive young lady that he thought he knew, but just could not place her until now.

"Is the Care Home investigation still ongoing?" asked Alan.

"Well, yes, it is. If you recall, your predecessor at the time asked for a full lesson learned review and update to policy and procedures that was done and came into effect last June."

Alan nodded his head. His stare drifted along the walls of the conference room to the large, framed photograph of the deceased Letty Stark. His mind drifted momentarily as he recalled the public rebuke that he had got from Letty at a time in the past. The memory still cut sharply in his mind.

He realized that negative events in the past dominate memory recall and influence how it is remembered. The more time spent on a negative memory, the more the recall is changed and tinged with certain biases, to eventually distort the memory.

The meeting room fell to silence as each of the Section Heads averted their eyes and pretended to scribble some important reminder notes into their journals.

Alan quickly got to his feet. His left arm jerked, causing him to grab his wrist with his right hand and appeared to seethe in pain. Sarah Ryan, who was still standing in her presenter position, noticed, and instinctively moved around the table towards Alan.

"Are you alright?" she asked, concerned.

By now, the other members had also risen as Alan's left side spasmed again.

"Leave him please, it will pass in a moment," said Sarah firmly. "I have seen this before with him."

Alan suddenly stood upright and glared at those around him. His wide eyes were almost outside his eye sockets and gave the appearance of a wild animal about to attack. His mind buzzed inside his brain as though an electrical shortage had fused across a connector somewhere deep in the recesses.

Alan recited numbers out loud, as though using them to calm

his raging mind. He reverted to a previous distraction method and counted a familiar Fibonacci sequence with ease and fluidity. It seemed to have the desired effect of calming, and soon his hand stopped the involuntary shaking and his expanded pupils returned to normal size.

In the privacy of an office, and not unlike a caring sibling, Sarah Ryan placed her arm across his shoulder and invited Alan to sit back down slowly in his seat. His frame was rigid. He seemed to struggle with bending his knees and holding his hip as though a person much older than his years.

"You have changed since our last meeting," said Alan softly in a low tone. His demeanor changed from wild and uncontrollable to tame and resigned. It was as though he was a different person. He felt a strange comfort with Sarah holding his arm as though blood family. The young girl who had once shared the love of poetry all those years ago was now like a sibling to Alan and a daughter to Letty Stark's mind.

Sarah looked straight at Alan and deep into his eyes that pierced like ice. She sensed a certain familiarity about the eyes. A familiarity that she had seen only in the eyes of her dear Letty Stark before her passing. The connection was brief enough to touch Sarah deeply as she recognized the eyes of her mentor and surrogate mother Letty Stark.

As the medical team entered the office and gathered around the patient, Sarah let go and stepped back to let them do their jobs. She could not help but stare back at eyes that looked at her, almost helpless. As though asking an unknown question of her.

'*What are you trying to say, Letty?*'

◆ ◆ ◆

TIME AND THE MIND

T wo thousand years ago, people walked the shifting path with no markers to follow or to point their direction. They looked at the sky and stars for guidance. A small boy was walking beside his older brother and asked, "Why are we looking up at the stars when all they do is look back at us, wondering the same?"

The older brother responded. "All men have the stars. For some, they are lights in the sky. For others, they are a guide to where we are going."

The attending doctor folded the cover of medical reports on Alan Irvenko and wiped the back of his hand across his forehead to clear the early forming drops of perspiration. DNA sequencing and blood tests confirmed Alan was a young man in his early thirties and all his biological functions supported that age diagnosis.

However, his brain scans showed clear evidence of dementia not expected for another forty or fifty years. Magnetic Resonance Imaging scans showed confirmed signs of beta plaque buildup, deep inside his brain, more common in someone eighty years of age and a marker of Alzheimer's disease. His urine test results showed unusual levels of Pyroluria present only in the most disturbed of mental patients. The consulting doctor was perplexed.

As part of the intensive care team associated with older adults resident in the respite home for terminal patients, he recognized the brain scans as those of a previous care patient that had passed some months previously. He was familiar with Letty Stark as a patient and was confused to see her scans mixed in with a much younger and arrogant patient. He re-checked the name of the medical file that read Alan Irvenko. He assumed the most rational explanation of clerical error in mixing the two files and summarily set the file aside on his desk. Less easy to set aside, the Doctor's concerns remained with him.

Later that afternoon, the consultant physician met with the rest of his colleagues at a closed-door meeting in the boardroom.

"This experiment has gone too far. If it gets out what was done here, we will face serious sanctions from the regulatory agency," opened a visibly agitated associate still in his white lab coat.

"Surely, we have plausible deniability. No one here sanctioned these trials. The responsible party passed away months ago."

"I don't think that will wash. We are all aware of what Letty Stark wanted to achieve and ignored her ethically questionable and self-indulgent experiments."

"Clearly, whatever early improvements that were achieved with brain resonance between the subjects is now reversing. The patients' behavioral patterns are becoming more erratic and unpredictable. The brain scans we have all seen show that Letty's aged mind is rewiring neural pathways in Alan's brain at a rate not seen before in clinical trials."

All the team members looked at each other with concern written in their eyes. There was no need to speak and no words to express the worry that each of them felt deep down inside.

All knew the repercussions that faced each of them personally. If there was a reset button for this trial, all would gladly push it.

The senior neurologist paced the room. The bespectacled man stared down at the carpet tiles as he strode up and down. He looked worried. One arm wrapped around his waist as though to hold in his middle-age spread, while the other hand attached to his chin as if to keep his head from falling off. Every few steps he shook his head from side to side, as though having an unspoken conversation with the carpet tiles. His hand straightened his head, and he continued his pace.

The room was silent. Terminating an experiment was one thing. However, Alan Irvenko was the experiment patient that was quickly determining his own path outside the control of those conducting the experiment. He was a breathing experiment and was oblivious to the discussions going on about him. Well, except for suspicion, perhaps. His psychosis told him frequently enough that his colleagues were discussing him behind his back, but his growing arrogance counteracted that he didn't need to care what anyone else thought of him.

Later that evening, Alan heard a voice in his mind. It was a voice that told him what he needed to do next.

Alan couldn't ignore the voice. It was commanding and demanding. He tried to resist, but the voice grew stronger and more insistent. It was telling him to prepare himself.

Get dressed now, insisted the internal voice.

Within twenty minutes, he dressed in an overcoat and headed out the apartment front door, not sure where he was going or why.

Like his ancient ancestors thousands of years ago, he felt like he was on a path that was laid out for him. One that he couldn't ignore.

As he walked, he looked up at the sky and the stars. They seemed to guide him, like a beacon in the dark. He remembered words from a distant memory, or a book he had read, about how the stars were looking back at those looking up. But now he saw them differently; perhaps they were a sign of hope and guidance, leading him towards his destiny.

"*THAT ISN'T* what I asked for," said Alan in a raised tone.

The rest of the bar stool members seated at the bar glanced towards the raised voice. But on seeing Alan sitting alone, and who was recognized as a regular, smiled and turned away, nursing their drinks intentionally.

The small narrow bar was crowded that Saturday afternoon. This was the post lunch crowd hanging on to the last drink before returning to their home and family lives.

Alan appeared to those around him to be having a conversation with himself.

"And what did you hear?"

That you weren't entirely blameless, for the matter.

"I most certainly was," responded Alan. "What are you suggesting?"

Don't forget, you can't fool me. I employed you once, and I know you far too well to be taken in by your antics.

"SHUT UP bitch–SHUT UP" shouted Alan, clenching fists on the bar top in visible anger.

By now, the other patrons sitting at the bar were listening with a feigned interest in the man talking to himself at the end of the counter, as no one had asked the barman for a drink for eight minutes. Some sniggered and others stared in open disbelief.

"Give him another of whatever he's drinking," shouted one of the bar stool audience while nodding toward Alan. "At least for the entertainment."

The bar man hesitantly obliged and placed a tumbler in front of Alan while pouring from a whisky bottle the desired measure. Alan did not react and instead mumbled to himself something indiscernible. A low muttering sound and a shaking of his head,

Alan's knuckles white from clenching. His eyelids remained closed but showed signs of rapid eye movement, as though in a deep sleep.

Do you remember my asking you after my funeral why people couldn't understand that the world has changed? Didn't that priest of God realize he is no better than us? I shall not forget your reply. He is, you said, far better than we deserve. I returned to my sleep that night angered by your selfish weakness.

Alan momentarily awoke from his invisible discussion and exchanged one empty tumbler glass for the full one sitting beside each other. Knocking the drink back in one gulp, he casually glanced around him as though becoming suddenly aware of the uninvited attention he was receiving from the lonely souls' club sharing the bar counter.

Inside, Alan's heart ached because he knew what was still to come. He had never thought to regret meeting his surrogate mother and still thought fondly of the old woman who had left him alone in this world of apathy and contempt. Deep inside, he knew she had not left him completely and part of her lived on inside his mind. He did not understand fully the mission assigned to him or why Letty had selected him, but determined at that point to follow the pattern as Letty had laid out for him.

THE LAST SUPPER

On the second day, an enormous snake slithered forward from its hole in the ground and blocked the path of the elder. "Why are you here walking in footsteps that are not yours?" asked the snake as it raised itself as high as it could. The elder stopped in fear and wondered for a moment how he should answer the snake's question, in case it should strike out at his response.

"You are sadly mistaken, for these footsteps are mine alone. I follow my path to a destination that is for each of us to decide."

Father Hansen and Sister Anne had just sat down for their evening meal later than usual. With the prayer before the meal said, each of the two servants of the church made the sign of the cross and opened their eyes again.

"Sister Anne, what a feast you have cooked up for us this evening," spoke Father Hansen as he rubbed his hands together. His eyes beamed greedily out across the feast laid out on a white linen cloth. He quickly leaned forward and carved.

"So," he said, "you were about to tell me why you kept the dedication cards from the old woman's funeral - the one signed by that strange man, Alan Irvenko?"

Sister Anne looked up, surprised at the directness of the question from her priest. She looked around the small empty room as though to check that no one else was listening.

"Would you kindly not make accusations over dinner in the parish house? God knows who might be listening. You need to learn to be more discreet in these matters. To express meaning without speaking so that others understand. It is God's wonder that you have risen to be a parish priest at such a tender age."

Father Hansen glanced at her for a moment in surprise as he placed his carved meat on his dinner plate. He was determined to get his share of the roast dinner first and converse second.

"Indeed. But I didn't mean to offend you," he said apologetically as he scooped a last spoon of peas to his plate.

Sister Anne was already chewing and so held her silence momentarily as she waited to swallow. There was something about the young priest's tone that she found annoying. The way he said, "offend you," as though slightly amused or just trying to be funny.

"No, I'm sorry," she said, "I have had a headache since earlier today and I might have responded short."

"You're still getting the headaches?" asked Father Hansen.

"Not so often," she responded. Her mind was clearly processing the response, while chewing on a piece of fat loudly.

"I read somewhere on the internet that too much exposure to artificial light can affect our circadian rhythms. It affects my sleep, and I get tiredness headaches."

Father Hansen lifted another mouthful to his mouth. A knock at the door turned his attention to annoyance at being disturbed at this evening hour. At that moment, he forgot that God's work is not done on set hours, and he set himself to ignore whoever it was calling at this hour.

"I'll get that," responded Sister Anne, accepting religious hierarchy and her place as a servant of God that sometimes extended to his representatives on earth.

The small nun swung open the wooden door and peered up at the large, looming presence of a man she recognized. He was dressed appropriately for this dark evening and held the collar of his dark coat across his face. His piercing eyes announced him without speaking. In that moment, she felt the presence of the snake on the path before her.

"Mr. Irvenko, sir, what on earth brings you out at this hour?"

Without speaking, Alan Irvenko stepped into the porch light and wiped his shoes on the small entrance mat printed with large red letters that read *God is Here.*

"For God's sake, who is it?" shouted the priest uncharacteristically from inside the house, just before he hurriedly shoved another fork of food into his mouth.

The sudden appearance of Alan Irvenko before him caused the priest to pause his chew and put down his cutlery. The priest swallowed hard to clear his throat and dabbed his mouth with the white linen napkin before rising to his feet to welcome an unwelcome guest to the table.

"Mr. Irvenko, what an unexpected pleasure! Please take off your coat and join us at our supper table," blurted the priest in rapid-fire speech mode.

The words sounded like they were falling from his mouth. As if he had lost control of his vocal cords and they were strumming away of their own free will. Laughing with hidden fear, perhaps.

Alan Irvenko was tall. He looked down at the small stature of a priest with a look of disdain on his face. That look when eyes look down while the mouth curls up at each end, as though holding in something held in the mouth. Alan's presence alone created a chill to be felt by anyone close to him.

"What can I do for you?" asked Father Hansen, bending slightly, and making himself even smaller, as though he was a small animal cowering in front of a predator. Hoping for mercy.

Irvenko put his two leather-gloved hands together, intertwining each finger as though to make the glove fingers fit tight. His long dark overcoat made him appear broader and taller, that made onlookers look down and away. For those who could look at his face long enough, they would see a clean-shaven square jawline, with prominent cheekbones protruding slightly, and recessed eye sockets shadowed by a high plateau of a forehead. His eyes looked as though crystal. As though they could see through you.

After an uncomfortable silence between the two men, Alan pulled one finger on his black leather gloves to expose a pale white hand that exposed the other gloved hand.

"Are you a man who watches life go by, or a participator that shapes his own life and that of others?" asked Alan in a slow, deliberate tone, as though speaking to someone who did not have English as their first language.

The philosophical nature of the question surprised Father Hansen, and he momentarily chewed his lips.

"Perhaps. Well... I mean, do you want a yes or no answer? I think I am both. I like to watch over my congregation with the view of providing guidance when it is needed."

Alan's rectangular-shaped head leaned to one side as though about to topple off his broad shoulders. His eyes trained on the priest.

"What have you achieved in your life that has added meaning to anyone else?"

"What?"

"What have you achieved, Priest?" this time slightly louder.

"I will answer that question for my Maker when He asks at the time of reckoning. But why are you asking?"

Alan Irvenko smiled. "I read a pattern in the sky tonight.

Positions of star formations concerning the position of the earth speak to me in a language that is not the privilege of others to understand."

A sudden jerk in Alan's left hand caused him to flex his hand. Spreading all five fingers wide as though exercising the nerves of his hand. His face winced in pain and then, as suddenly as it had appeared, the pain subsided.

"Are you in pain?" asked the priest, stating the obvious.

"I have some trouble, yes. A nagging nerve in my arm keeps me awake at night like a demanding child when it needs attention. I am not immune to the aging gene that has slowly crept up on me and now taunts me from a safe distance. But I have a good relationship with pain. It reminds me I am still alive. A small price to pay for the privilege, don't you think?"

"The privilege is life itself, and we should expect no more than we receive from our Creator." said the Priest.

The frail-looking priest gave the semblance of a smile.

Sister Anne stood just a small distance back from the two men until the priest made eye contact with her, signaling her to step closer.

"Let me take your coat, Mr. Irvenko, and please take a seat at our table," she interjected, clasping her hands before her as though about to lead a prayer group.

Alan Irvenko pursed his lips momentarily as though thinking about where and what seat he should take. He extended his good right arm to offer over his overcoat and eventually sat down. The priest followed suit and seemed happier as the seated positions diminished the standing height disadvantage.

"So, to what do we owe the honor of your visit, Mr. Irvenko?" asked the priest, as though speaking to one of his repentant parishioners.

Alan surveyed the food on the table. His hesitancy was deliberate, as though thinking about his response, or perhaps just deciding what to select from the food choice before him.

"Recently, I have experienced a recurring dream that has disturbed my night pattern. It appears to me most nights and I see the aging face of a departed colleague who I feel may have a message to communicate. I would like your assistance to contact the recently deceased Letty Stark, whom I believe you both know?"

Both the nun and the priest glanced momentarily at each other before turning back to their dinner guest.

"You want us to help you contact the deceased Letty Stark?" asked the priest hesitantly. Surprise mixed with disbelief clouded his thoughts as the priest tried to comprehend what his guest was asking.

Undeterred, Alan lifted a small silver fork to his mouth and placed the forked morsel of cooked meat into it. Slowly, closing his mouth, extracting the metallic instrument to leave the food inside. His jaws processed the meat in a rhythmic motion while savoring the taste.

Eventually, Alan swallowed and placed his fork on the table, while dabbing a pristine napkin to his mouth with his other hand.

"I have heard the voice of Letty Stark in my mind for some time now, and even more so since her passing. This bitch haunts my thoughts day and night. We, or specifically you, will help me put her to rest for the last time."

Neither the priest nor the nun answered, instead choosing to look down at the white tablecloth to avert their eyes and buy themselves time. Eventually, as though an act of distraction, Sister Ann reached forward and picked up the white gravy jug and poured some over her plate until it nearly overflowed.

The silence between Father Hansen and Alan Irvenko stretched out, each man sizing up the other. Sister Anne watched them both warily, sensing the tension that hung in the air.

"I'm not sure I understand the question," Father Hansen finally replied, his voice betraying his unease.

Alan Irvenko leaned forward; his hands still clasped together. "Are you content to simply watch the world go by, to let things happen around you, or do you actively shape your own life and the lives of those around you?"

"I believe I try to make a difference in the lives of my congregation and those in the community," Father Hansen said, still uncertain where this conversation was heading.

"Do you really?" Alan Irvenko asked, leaning forward with an elbow on the table, his tone sounding sceptical. "Or are you content to merely maintain the status quo, to uphold tradition and ritual without truly challenging or changing anything?"

Father Hansen opened his mouth to reply, but no words came out. He realized with a start that there was some truth to what Alan Irvenko was saying. Perhaps he had fallen into a routine, content to simply go through the motions of his duties without questioning whether there was more he could do to help his congregation.

"I think you need to leave now," Sister Anne interjected, breaking the uncomfortable silence. Her voice was firm. "It's not appropriate for you to be here at this hour, and I don't like the way you're speaking to Father Hansen."

Alan Irvenko ignored her, his gaze fixed on the young priest. "You have a choice," he said. "You can continue on the path you're on, or you can choose to forge a fresh path, one that challenges you and those around you to be better, to do more."

"I think you should go," Father Hansen said, standing up and gesturing towards the door. "Thank you for your... advice."

Alan held the sharp meat knife in his right hand. He noticed the carved intricate handle that contained symbols of religious belief. His left hand placed the fork on the table.

Alan Irvenko rose to his feet, his eyes never leaving Father Hansen's face.

"Remember what I said," his voice was low. "There is more to life than just going through the motions."

Sister Anne also rose to her feet. The small stature of a woman dwarfed by the towering Alan Irvenko. She stepped towards Alan as though to show the urgency to leave as requested. Alan casually dropped his look from the priest to look down on the small woman looking up at him. Although her mouth was moving, Alan could not hear any words coming from her. With a quickness of strength, he turned the nun by her shoulders so that her back was to him and he placed both hands on her exposed neck, restraining her from turning back. Her intuitive response was to grab at both his arms. With his physical strength, he pulled the nun closer so that she could feel his power over her. Leaning slightly forward, he breathed in deeply and exhaled onto her white soft exposed neckline. She could smell his tobacco breath that increased her terror state.

Father Hanson saw the terror in the eyes of his servant's assistant. He felt paralysed and afraid to move.

As Sister Anne's breathing became more constrained, her mouth opened wide, gasping to breathe. As she did so, Alan's hands closed ever tighter until the struggle to breathe stopped. Still holding the throat of the small woman, he positioned his face to look at hers. Eyes wide with open mouth, he considered for a moment her last thoughts. As he loosened his stranglehold, he felt the weight of the woman crumple to the carpet floor beneath.

Father Hanson dropped to his knees in front of them, reaching out an arm with hand trembling in mid-air towards the crumpled-up presence on the floor.

"Oh my God, what have you done? What have you done?" repeated the Priest over and over.

With that, Alan had already picked up his dark overcoat and deftly slipped one arm into the sleeve while swinging the rest of the jacket over his shoulder to attend to the other arm. He turned and strode towards the door, his coat tails billowing behind him. The two remaining in the room enveloped by the cries and shouts from the priest calling on the deaf ears of a master's higher power to intervene.

Just as Alan got to the hallway, a voice he recognized screamed his name and Alan stopped in his tracks. It was the voice of Sarah Ryan.

Calmly, she stood before Alan.

"What have you done?"

Alan looked behind to the kneeling priest over the body of the nun. At that moment, Alan felt a familiar sharp pain run from his left arm that made him wince. Grabbing his left arm, he snapped his head from side to side as the pain sharpened and then ebbed. Alan's conscious mind engaged, and he came back into the reality of the moment.

Alan's expression changed from rage to desperation as he quickly understood the gravity of the circumstances developing around him. The priest was on his knees and wailed over the slumped dark body of the nun sprawled across the blood-soaked carpet floor.

Sarah Ryan surveyed the scene of utter hopelessness. She whispered in a faint voice what sounded like a poem or perhaps a prayer. In front of her, with his back turned to them, the priest on his knees, holding the hand of the dead nun to his cheek, rocking back and forth. The brightly lit room was full of sound. From the priest wailing on the floor to voices talking indiscernibly. Almost a jumble of voices, with each talking over the other. Sarah smiled and felt the handle of the knife in her hand.

"Finish what you have started," came a voice over the others.
"What are you waiting for?"
"Do it now."

Sarah glanced down at her right hand to see that she was

holding the beautiful ornate knife still in her blood-soaked hand. Looking back to the priest, she stepped forward and mentally timed the movement of the priest as he rocked back and forward on his knees. She hesitated and then placed one arm across the forehead of the priest to expose his throat and with the other drew the knife blade across the pale exposed skin in a quick deliberate action. Releasing the arm lock, the priest slumped forward on his own weight, his head landing on the chest of the nun beneath him. Blood gushed from the sliced Adam's apple of the priest's throat and soaked into the carpet floor.

The voices got louder inside Alan's head. Each voice talking over the other to make sense impossible before finally quieting.

"Wait," called Sarah's voice, breaking the silence.

"Letty, is it you?"

"It's total bullshit, and none of this applies to me. I am not a fuckin' psychopath," responded the voice of Letty Stark to the silence of the room.

"It was God's calling," answered Alan back. "Place them on the bed in the bedroom next door and they will sleep more comfortably."

After dragging both bodies from the dining room via a small hallway to a small darkened bedroom, Alan had placed both bodies on top of the duvet cover and sat down on the foot of the bed as if to catch his breath. Turning back to the bodies, he reached across and emptied the trouser pocket of the priest and placed the contents on the bed next to him. A tissue paper and a small holy medal, the entire pocket content.

On the 28th May 1996, Alan Irvenko and unknown others had called on the parish priest home of Father Hansen and Sister Anne. Having murdered them both using a kitchen knife, placed both bodies on to a bed and set the parish house ablaze.

That night, just like the first predicted Solar Eclipse of the Grecian Island of Miletus in 585 BC, darkness spanned again across a swath of the earth. Perhaps this time, the darkness was man made and little to do with God or Nature.

THE AGE GENE

Some weeks later, Letty Stark's mind, in the physical form of Alan Irvenko, sat on the front porch veranda and pondered aging life. Perhaps destiny has brought us to where we are right now, at this exact moment. That we have no control over life events. Perhaps it is fate that controls our destiny, and we are simply passengers along for the ride. If this is true, then we really have nothing to worry about as life finds its own path for us.

Over recent times, advances in the understanding of hygiene, disease eradication, and food availability combined with improved living standards have resulted in extended life for much of the so called developed world populations. Over the last century, it has almost doubled from forty-five years to eighty-five years. However, there is no pre-defined limit on age. There are other mammals, such as Bowhead Whales, which can live up to two hundred and eleven years, or an ocean Quahog species that lives for four hundred years!

Curiously, by 2024, no specific gene has been identified that triggers the biological countdown clock. This means we are not doomed to die from the moment we are born. Rather, humans develop this countdown clock through a complex interplay of lifestyle choices and environmental factors. These influences collectively determine when the biological countdown will start.

From the moment we are born, our bodies embark on a journey of growth and development, marked by various stages of maturation. Initially, we undergo rapid physical and cognitive development, reaching several milestones along the way. During childhood and adolescence, our biological systems focus on growth, repair, and optimizing bodily functions. A remarkable capacity for resilience and recovery characterizes this period of life.

As we transition into adulthood, our bodies reach a state of maturity where the rate of growth slows, and biological processes begin to stabilize. It is during this phase that our biological systems enter a sort of stasis, maintaining equilibrium to ensure optimal functioning. This stasis period can last for many years, during which our bodies continue to perform efficiently, provided we maintain a healthy lifestyle and avoid harmful environmental influences.

However, this state of biological balance is not permanent. Over time, various factors can disrupt this equilibrium, initiating the aging process. These factors can include genetic predispositions, environmental exposures, lifestyle choices, and even random cellular events. For example, prolonged exposure to harmful environmental factors such as pollution, radiation, or toxins can damage cellular structures and accelerate aging. Similarly, unhealthy lifestyle choices such as poor diet, lack of exercise, smoking, and excessive stress can also contribute to the breakdown of biological processes and hasten the onset of aging.

Moreover, the body's ability to repair and regenerate itself diminishes with age. Cellular damage accumulates over time, and the efficiency of repair mechanisms declines. This leads to the gradual deterioration of tissues and organs, manifesting as the physical and cognitive changes associated with aging. The rate at which these changes occur can vary widely among individuals, influenced by both genetic and environmental factors.

Interestingly, recent research has suggested that certain interventions may help delay the onset of the aging process and extend the period of stasis. For instance, maintaining a balanced diet rich in nutrients, engaging in regular physical activity, managing stress, and avoiding harmful substances can all contribute to healthier aging. Advances in medical science and technology also hold promise for mitigating some of the adverse effects of aging, potentially extending human lifespan and improving the quality of life in later years.

In conclusion, no single gene triggers the biological countdown clock, but the onset of aging is a complex process influenced by a combination of genetic, environmental, and lifestyle factors. As Letty lifted her eyes from reading, she pondered this life-changing moment; she wondered to herself what was the trigger point in her own life that had started her aging clock countdown. What could she have done differently knowing now the devastating consequences a lifestyle choice made in ignorance would have on her future life?

External conditions, such as a heavily processed diet, lifestyle, environmental exposures, disease, injuries, all contribute to, or at least influence, our RNA / DNA sequence. Once genetically introduced, the cells replicate, and the countdown clock begins to tick. And Letty knew the tick only got louder with time.

Unfortunately, the one organ that has not kept up with the trend of longer lifespans is the human brain. This remarkable organ, which is complex, mysterious, self-communicating, adaptive, and self-learning, lags in terms of its resistance to aging. Dementia, in all its forms, remains a significant medical challenge. To some extent, society accepts dementia as a normal part of aging. It is often perceived as an inevitability of getting old, as if our memory centers have a different lifespan and have not caught up with our extended biological lifespans. Science is still trying to understand why the undetected symptoms of Alzheimer's can develop twenty years before symptoms are present and an actual diagnosis can be determined, and sadly, there is still little to no medical intervention to prevent its progression.

Given this dark and depressing scenario of living longer with a deteriorating mind that cannot remember, that cannot learn, that cannot sustain its own host body, and does not enjoy or value life. Perhaps some people do not live longer than they are supposed to simply because they do not want to? In their minds, they decide they are done. Life's purpose is over for them. Without meaning, life becomes mundane and a drudgery as each day and each week rolls into the next.

Letty Stark understood that her brain was aging, and that there was little or nothing she could do to hold back the march of time. Glancing down at her physical bodily host, she could not help but marvel at the physicality of Alan Irvenko. Maintaining his fitness, he had kept in shape. She felt a physical arousing in her thoughts that she had not felt for a long time.

Thinking back to her time in the nursing home for the aged and physically infirm, each day is determined only by the routine of a sequence of pills to take. Blue and red in the morning. Green and yellow at lunchtime, another red and blue before bedtime. As though colored pills take a defining role, somehow setting a living pattern for the aged mind to follow.

"What day is it again?"
"Did I take my pills already?"

Sarah mentioned to Letty almost sarcastically that complaining also seems to be a common symptom of old age. It is an affliction that many take too easily that gives a sort of meaning to life for those that have none or feel that they are simply clinging to life. Waiting for the inevitable. On simple terms, complaining is just a way for the mind to find a purpose to interact with others when their life purpose has changed, or perhaps because their original life purpose is already achieved or, sometimes, sadly, lost. Parent roles evaporate, caregivers become the cared for. Gradually, life roles change.

Of course, there are those that will sustain a healthy mind combined with healthy aging. They maintain a positive attitude; they have interests and feel that they have a purpose still left in their lives.

Is it just fantasy that we can live longer? mused Letty as she closed her eyes, drifting off to sleep.

On the other side of this coin reality, Alan Irvenko's mind was spiraling downward, and he was losing control of his thoughts as his consciousness slowly but surely merged with the aged brain of Letty Stark. He fought to control his thoughts as he felt the lack of control take him to dark recesses in his subconscious. But the possession of Alan's body with the mind of Letty Stark was near complete.

Alan winced as his left arm tingled again in pain. He had noticed that whenever this happened, he would black out for a while, entering the dream state. Present in his body and aware, but it would seem like he was daydreaming. He also noticed how the pain was extending past his arm up through his shoulder to a point behind his left ear and into his brain. The pain was excruciating and incapacitating.

Although he did not know how, Alan attributed the pain to Letty, reaffirming his need to exorcise this woman from his mind.

That following morning, Alan walked purposely into the company's main entrance with a set mission in his mind. He followed his usual surveyance ritual and was pleased that everything was nearly as it should be. Alan observed a perceptible slowdown in travel speed for the lift and made a mental note to contact the maintenance office to deal with the problem again as soon as possible.

Alan sat in his seat at an elevated position. The scientists studied him as if waiting for him to generate a second head. His extreme confidence was borderline arrogance.

"I want full control of my body back. You will retract the parasite in my head. I no longer want to be her host," he said firmly, glaring at everyone seated around the table, as if daring someone to speak against him.

"We would have to conduct some tests first, Mr. Irvenko to ensure that it is safe," the senior associate said to him calmly.

Alan slammed his fists on the table hard. "Then do so immediately after this meeting!" he growled.

Alan stayed later than usual in his office that night, working on reports of projects that had been submitted, and his head felt woozy. The tingling sensation in his left arm forewarned what was to come. And as inevitable as it was, the firebolt fired up his left arm into his brain just behind his left ear. Alan winced and involuntarily flexed as the inevitable brain fog descended.

"Alan..." he heard his name called inside his mind. He looked up and out of his glazed office door across the darkened open plan office; the office desks are empty. He went on with his work, hoping against hope that his imagination was playing tricks on him, and he was just being paranoid.

"Don't ruin my life's work, Alan," the voice whispered. The female soft tone diluted by a menacing undercurrent that tiptoed around the words and around the neuronal pathways inside Alan's head.

Alan Irvenko's heart raced. "L-Letty?" He stuttered as he recognized the voice, and he spun around in his office as if expecting to see a physical form to the voice.

"You fool!" she yelled in response, sending him to his knees as a sharp pain shot through his autonomic nerves.

He winced in pain, curling up on the ground as he affirmed what he already knew, that the voice was from inside his head. She was slowly but surely gaining control inside him.

"This is my body," he spat in pain, his eyes red as blood, the veins in his head popping out as though they would tear through the skin, a shrill ringing noise in his ear, *tinnitus*...

"I shall tear you down, nerves to nerves, veins to veins, limbs to limbs," she threatened, daring him ahead of the future if he tried to rid her from his mind.

The pain subsided after a few minutes; Alan got off the floor drenched in his own sweat and dropped back into his office seat.

"Letty, I am not sure that I can deliver your expectations."

"Stop complaining and do what I say. Remember, from here forward, I am you and you are me. Act like it and stop resisting what is already done."

Alan did not respond. He did not know what to say and stayed silent. Moments passed before Alan eventually got to his feet. His legs and body vibrated as he moved as hastily as he could. He shut down his computer and put it inside his briefcase.

Using his cell phone, he hastily sent a text message without checking it twice to his science research team. He didn't care how strange it looked or how insane it might make him appear. It was science that put that bitch into his head, and it will be science who will remove her.

Early the following morning, the research geneticists had assembled at the science lab and prepared their patient for the tests ahead. As the team ran tests on Alan, he felt the pain intensify, and he realized Letty's presence strengthening in his mind. Blood samples taken from Alan were rushed through the various processing steps to filter and collect the t-cells and wash out impurities, leaving pure genetic code. The genetic biologists identified unusual cell markers that promoted rapid intracellular communication and also the clear presence of female specific markers that they would not expect to find in males.

However, he did not have to wait long before the tests revealed that Letty's age damaged DNA had fused with his own. They were now a single entity. Alan was both horrified and fascinated at the same time.

Was this what fate had in store for him? Was this his destiny?

After further days of intense clinical research into Alan's harvested cell samples, they discovered that the Alan and Letty combined cells had a unique genetic structure. The cells showed a strong resilience and appeared to multiply much faster than normal replication almost twice as fast as comparable healthy cell samples. In addition, and despite normal age-related cell damage, they discovered the DNA sample could sustain life beyond normal expected age span, and it was now a part of Alan's genetic code. He would now have the ability to live for at least a century. They also recognized that the discovery had the potential to be ground-breaking and could revolutionize the medical world and the treatment of aging.

Later that afternoon, Alan received a debriefing and processed the results presented to him by his research team with mixed emotions. He understood the advantage of a slowed genetic clock and what this could potentially mean, not just for him but for wider society.

Alan had always been ambitious, but he now felt that he had a new purpose in life. He hoped at least that he could use his newfound abilities to make a difference in the world. He believed he could achieve anything he set his mind to, and he was determined to do so. His mind was sharper, and he could now process information faster than ever before. He was more resilient to disease, and his body, or at least his mind, was regenerating cells at an accelerated rate. Simply put, he could think faster if he could keep Letty's mind in the background.

Alan stared at the ceiling above his room and pondered what his future might be as the inevitable calling card triggered a sharp pulse of pain through his left arm to focus his attention.

"You will never get rid of me," hissed the voice of Letty inside his brain.

Over the following months, the business world and, in his own mind, Alan had become a research maverick. A trailblazer in genetics, cell therapy and intracellular communication. Thanks to the guidance of both Letty Stark and Sarah Ryan, Alan had pushed the boundaries of what was thought to be possible and had changed the world forever. As he looked back on his life, he realized perhaps fate had a plan for him, and he was simply a passenger along for the ride. But it was up to him to take control and shape his destiny.

Perhaps the human lifespan could reach unprecedented heights, and with Alan's help and the combined minds of Letty Stark and Sarah Ryan, the mysteries of aging could finally be unlocked. His contribution to humanity would be immeasurable, and his legacy would live on long after he was gone. Alan Irvenko felt that he had become immortal, and in doing so, at least in his own mind, he had become a symbol of hope for generations to come.

SPLITTING PERSONALITY

Alan and Letty were both aware that uncontrollable violence appeared to stem from multiple personality disorders (MPD) and linked to psychopathy that they would need to address to maintain stability. MPD applies to approximately 1% of the population with prevalence in males. Symptoms of MPD include seeking constant approval and validation from others who are successful in positions of power. Many are selfish and pathological liars with inflated egos and self-esteem. This self-inflated sense of importance is often contrasted with the reality that they might never amount to much and live a standard and boring existence of disappointment. This description resonated sharply with Alan Irvenko.

Alan was convinced he was smarter and more intelligent than he actually was. Often exaggerating his experience and accomplishments, he could not allow himself to be seen as inferior in the eyes of those he engaged with. In the rare cases where this situation arose, Alan would drift into severe depression with potentially violent rages imminent. A self defense coping mechanism is referred to as 'splitting' that separates out the ideal self from the actual self. It is a confused internal struggle between fantasy dreams of success and the greater fear of failure.

In Alan's case, this materialized in the distinct personalities of Letty Stark, to whom Alan attributed all his failures and Sarah Ryan, who he attributed to guiding success and empathy. In recent times, Alan was starting to resent the presence of Letty Stark in his thoughts and believed she was responsible for all the misfortune that had recently entered his life.

During one of these random depression episodes that induced sleep disturbance and eventually rage, Letty as Alan, took a loaded firearm from the lock cabinet and strolled out into the night looking to ease deep seated rage. It was a damp early morning at 3 am. Alan walked into a known homeless shelter area and hoped to exercise his pent up rage. A young teenage soul approached in a semi drugged state with make-up beyond her years unsuspecting of her fate. She willingly approached the well-dressed, affluent white male and thought perhaps an opportunity for her to make quick money.

The stranger was dressed to elicit attention and not for the weather conditions. Alan looked at her up and down for a minute as though to absorb the engagement presented before him. Not exactly what he was looking for, but it will suffice, he thought.

Loaded with modified hollow point ammunition, the weapon was a 9mm semi-automatic. The first and fatal shot was in near proximity to the face and split her head in two. The second two shots were fired into the abdomen as though to ensure death, demonstrating pre-mediated intention to kill.

Alan later described this killing to his confidant, and alternate personality, Sarah Ryan, as a terrible mistake. He recalled in great but false detail a night out for dinner and afterward returned to Alan's apartment where his 'new girlfriend' proceeded to take a phone call on her cell phone. She was laughing and joking and then suddenly Alan heard the voices in his head telling him how foolish he looked. His explosive response resulted in the violent rage that took the life of a young woman.

Sarah Ryan was not surprised at the story told. She was more concerned that Alan's recollection of the event had an elaborate story built up around it. Almost as if Alan was creating a soap opera in his head that he believed he was living.

"Alan, what restaurant did you go to that night?" asked Sarah calmly, probing his memory.

"Why are you calling me Alan?"

"Are you not Alan Irvenko?" she asked again, perplexed.

In his dark glazed eyes that reflected thunder clouds on a distant prairie rolling across the night sky, he felt the soft hand of Sarah touch his face, and his eyes focused on hers. Her scent permeated his senses and, in his mind, he saw an enormous field of yellow sunburst flowers.

"Sarah–I am glad to see you again–Where have you been?"

Sarah stared into the dark eyes. Wide and glistening. Inquisitive but sensitive at the same time. She heard and felt the shallow, fast breathing against her exposed skin.

"Where did you go?" came the voice again. This time more firm, but absolutely recognizable.

"Letty-is that really you?"

◆ ◆ ◆

RELIGIOUS PROTOCOL

By the cold calculus of survival, Homo Sapiens are the dominant species and still propagating the environment that we live in. In 2024, there are 44,000 animal and plant species listed under the Endangered Species list. According to the IUCN, this represents 28% of all species on earth and is growing. Despite increasing wars and rising obesity, humans are not on the list.

Combined with advances in pharmaceutical development driven largely by financial gain, we have recently found ways to suppress hunger through manipulation and targeting of GLP-1 hormones in the brain. This chemical suppression of a specific hormone helps to keep our weight in check that still enables us to eat high sugar content processed foods. We have found drugs and technology that will extend the human life span even further. Humans are now at risk of overrunning the entire planet, pushing many other species out of their natural habitat. It is therefore not a surprise that our dominance enables humans to make our own habitat, usually at the expense of other living species. Climate change, natural disasters, epidemics and exhaustion of natural resources push the balance even more in favor of one species at the cost of all others.

Yet, despite all our technological advances, deep inside our ancient brains, we are still hunter gatherers. The brain that enables us to write orchestral music and solve complex geometrical equations that put us into space has changed little in thousands of years.

We are, as we have been for thousands of years, still engaged in constant conflict, usually triggered by nothing more than cultural differences. In recent years, we have developed technology to enable the destruction and death of more and more people and the natural habitat of thousands of species.

"Is there a God who will forgive what we have done?" asked Letty.

"Who knows," responded Sarah. "But why would a God choose to speak through one person and not another?"

"I would like to be brought to a religious intervention to challenge where we are now and find out if extending human life is what our purpose really is. Is it what humanity needs right now?"

"That could be problematic, Letty, given what we have done and where we are now with the mind transfer vault. I don't think Alan is going to agree and his uncontrollable anger is, well, uncontrollable."

Sarah felt the sudden strength of the host catch her throat and squeeze hard. She felt her breathing restrict and instinctively held the wrists of the strong binding arms that inflicted pressure on her throat. "I'm not asking," growled the voice into the purple face of Sarah before finally releasing the grip.

Later that evening, the priest sanctified the room with holy water, preparing it for the exorcism of the host, Alan Irvenko.

The priest wasn't feeling up to the task, but felt it was his duty, bestowed upon him by some higher power. His predecessor never had to, but he had imparted the ancient religious protocol to them as part of their training and indoctrination to God's army.

Sarah explained to the religious zealots gathered it was a scientific experiment that Letty had been working on to combat a cognitive decline in aging. She explained to the celebrant that she didn't expect Letty would be alive inside him, controlling his thoughts, his mind, his very essence. It was more of him having her knowledge and experience before her memory completely faded.

What had failed was the understanding that the taking of the mind means that the soul is still connected. The soul is one's true self and acts as the bond that holds all the human parts consciously and unconsciously together. Letty, and her researchers, had either made an error in their calculations, or had intentionally omitted the information that fusing another person's mind with another could lead to possession. After all, this was the first type of mind transference experiment, and she had kept it just for herself, knowing she was going to die anyway.

Still, Sarah mused, Letty had done her homework. She must have known that the mind was more powerful than anyone else thought. She studied the law of attraction; they had mirrored Alan's feelings to stay in line with him for some weeks before and studied how to manipulate his thoughts. He thought they were his ideas, his thoughts floating through his mind.

The thing about Letty was also her undying desire and obsession with time and controlling it. This desire energized her. It didn't make her stay quiet inside of Alan.

Human beings are an intrinsic fragment of the universe. Everything we do, think, or say affects our environment, even if we do not see it. This study was the reason for Letty's climb to success on mind transference, preserve consciousness and to live longer.

The human brain is more developed than we think or comprehend. But we don't use up to half of it. This living computer is divided into consciousness and subconsciousness. However, nobody really pays attention to their subconscious mind. Except for Letty. She paid attention to her subconscious. That voice buried deep in your mind that you hear whisper occasionally but are quick to forget. She tapped into that power and wondered at the amazing things the human mind can do.

The attending priest didn't understand why he had to undo the error science had made and was only present out of duress.

"Place both hands, Alan, on the table in front of you. Palms facing down, please," asked the priest in a soft tone of voice that only the condescending have. His obedient assistant buzzed around, placing candles strategically on the white linen-clothed table.

The younger assistant was a willing servant and a true bride of Christ. She made her vows at an early age with no thought or hesitance. It was a family thing and an expectation that as the oldest daughter, she would keep the family tradition and join the Catholic service to provide and give back to others. It was like a mission. The young nun in training never really thought she had a choice in the matter, and her devotion was almost without thought. Everyone expected it to be that way. And she duly surrendered herself up to the service of God for the better of others.

"In the name of Jesus Christ, our God and Lord, strengthened by the intercession of the Immaculate Virgin Mary, Mother of God," echoed through the sacristy.

The congregation gathered, hung on every word recited by the priest, who spoke the words of their master, their God. Heads bowed in reverence; the religious sermon continued the verse recital.

"His enemies are scattered and those who hate him flee before him. As smoke is driven away, so are they driven. As wax melts before the fire, so the wicked perish at the presence of God."

And as the Priest continued with his prayers, Alan, with Letty and Sarah inside his head, sat there feeling nothing except irritation from the burning incense that teared up his eyes.

"You know what? I don't think this is working..." Alan finally said in an indignant tone.

The Priest looked at him quizzically, trying to decipher whether it was a possessed Alan talking.

"Alan. Do you hear me?"

Alan shook his head momentarily.

Then louder. "Alan!"

This time, Alan raised his head and opened his eyes wide. He breathed deep through nostrils and exhaled slowly, as if to calibrate his hearing.

"I know you hear me," called the familiar voice of Letty that he recognized with no doubt. Still, he hesitated. Perhaps hoping that it was just another trick of his damaged mind. Stretching his left hand wide open, he felt the familiar sharp pain through his left wrist that served only to confirm what he already knew.

He blinked his eyes and took in his surroundings. The front dining room of the priest's house was gone. Instead, he was seated in a small room of dull orange paint with no discernable features. Looking first right, then left, he felt the constraints of the small room and wondered. Afraid of what was behind him. He waited as though expecting.

"It's time to turn the tide. I need to learn to love you less," called the voice inside his mind. "It's time to let you go."

"What do you want of me? I have already delivered my side of the agreement. Why are you tormenting me like this?"

"Alan, say my name so that I know you know who I am."

"Letty, Letty, Letty. What do you want from he?" he shouted out.

"I am done with you and your mind games. We need to end

this and move on."

Alan felt his heart rate increase, and a coldness fell about him. Not fear. No. This was a presence that he could feel, as though someone standing too close to him. Threatening.

Another sharp shock from his left wrist up to his shoulder. This caused him to wince in the chair in pain. He automatically responded to the pain by grabbing his left wrist and dropping his head to look at the floor between his feet.

"Holy fuck!" he cried out, followed by a deep intake of air.

As the pain subsided, Alan repositioned himself upright in the seat. He rolled his shoulders and moved his head from side to side.

"You really should get that wrist seen to," said Letty in a slightly sarcastic tone. "It appears to me to be getting worse."

Alan sucked through his teeth as a dismissive gesture, feeling rage rising in his pre-frontal cortex. "Just tell me what you want, and we can all move on with our lives," he stuttered out. He then asked, sounding almost annoyed, "What is it?"

He suddenly felt the splashes of water on his face that momentarily startled him. An unfamiliar voice sounded. "I bind your unclean spirit," the voice of the celebrant continued, splashing more water on the red-faced man.

"Fuck!" Alan yelled in pain while rocking the chair back and forth.

The Priest recited a prayer in Latin before being interrupted again.

"Nothing is happening, Father," Alan said to the priest, as if trying to convince him. Alan wasn't feeling anything, except the water being continuously splashed on him and the incense choking him and stinging his eyes.

By now, the priest was more than happy to stop and be rid of the man and possibly the women inside of him.

As Alan left the priest's residence on that dusky evening, he again felt the familiar sharp shock run through his left arm. He grabbed his wrist with his right hand before releasing and shaking his arm vigorously. A sharp intake of breath to ease the pain.

What the fuck is happening now? He thought in his mind.

The sharpness of the pain seared his brain. Like an electrical charge from his left arm through his shoulder, to that deep sensitive point behind his left ear. The gateway to his brain. He winced at the pain that shot through his mind. For a moment, he saw flashes of white light across his eyes and heard a familiar voice whisper.

"I have worn you out, dear. It's showing on your face," spoke the familiar voice of Letty deep in the mind of the tormented Alan. "Surely now you know I need to let you go. When I look in the mirror and see your reflection, I can't stomach what I see."

A neuronal signal fired deep behind the pre-frontal cortex of Alan's brain to activate the amygdala, the most ancient and oldest part of the human brain. Of course, this occurs in the realms of the subconscious mind, without choice. A residual of ancient human instinct to survive that triggers the fight-or-flight response of the consciousness.

That night, Letty was free to do what she pleased. She felt her primal instincts and animal urges setting aside humanity as she headed out into the dark, damp night air. She relished the physicality of the youthful, strong, angry Alan Irvenko as a tool to do her bidding. An opportunity she intended to use tonight.

REVERSING THE SPIRAL

J oan was a slender and attractive lady in her early thirties who worked at the cash register in Bernie's, a local convenience store in the neighbourhood. She always brought her A-game to her job, if ever that was possible for a checkout attendant. But Joan was sweet. There was something inviting and wholesome about her. She was friendly and would talk to anyone who looked her way twice. A daydreamer, she was comfortable in her own thoughts and often wished away time before bouncing back into the reality of her mundane existence.

But who decides what is a mundane life? Joan was content. She saw her life working on some higher purpose, serving others, providing company, for those who came into her small world and her circle of existence.

Letty Stark, when she had her own body, and before her dementia had taken hold, would often come into the store to buy food supplies or office utilities. This usually comprised tea or coffee or a pencil or a ruler. Never really any sense to the purchase, and Joan let herself believe it was loneliness reaching out for comfort. Joan had dealt with Letty on more than one occasion and felt she knew the old woman well. Her visits connected with Joan's higher purpose in life to serve the community.

However, Letty would be unnecessarily rude to the shopkeeper, and Joan had had about enough of the elderly woman and demanded respect as a human being.

Letty had laughed in her face scornfully, like Joan was deluded, so Joan had turned Letty out of the store that day and told her not to return until she could mind her manners.

Some days later, Letty had come back to lodge a complaint, hoping that the disrespecting young woman would get fired. But all Letty had gotten in return was a standard query letter from the head office, which disappointed and pissed off Letty; the woman didn't like to lose and vowed revenge.

Months passed, and the incident with Letty faded into the background of Joan's life. She continued her routine, finding solace in the small interactions she had with regular customers. Her dreams still played in her mind, and she often found herself lost in thought, imagining a life filled with excitement and adventure, far removed from the confines of Bernie's Convenience Store.

One rainy evening, Joan was engrossed in a book. The world outside was a blur of grey. The door bell chimed, signalling that someone had entered the store. Joan set her book down and got up from her seat to deal with the customer.

"Welcome to Bernie's. How may I help you?" she asked, before looking up and in an automatic sounding tone.

Suddenly, Joan let out a deafening scream as the person charged at her, jumping swiftly over the counter as though previously trained to do so. A heavy blow landed on the side of Joan's face, followed by another and another. The striking blows relentless.

Her masked assaulter pulled out a large sheathed knife and placed a hand over her mouth so her cries would be muffled. With what strength she had left, Joan's slight frame fought back. Her arms, her hands, her legs, flayed wildly, as though a machine trying to gather up dust.

"Here's to levelling the score," the voice whispers gently, piercing the knife into her neck, while severing the vocal chords and major arteries.

Half of the knife went in, but whoever it was wasn't satisfied and would not take any chances of Joan surviving.

Joan's body jerked back and forth as she tried to fight off the assailant. She clawed her hands at her assailant's face in a frenzy of desperation, overcome by the strength of a person with intent.

The attacker was on a mission and was going to finish the task. Using the other hand, the attacker forcefully jammed the knife all the way into Joan's neck. Followed by a successive pattern of knife stabs repeating exactly 11 times. With each stab wound, time slowed for Joan. She sensed a strange familiarity from her attacker. She knew she knew this person who had done her harm. But inevitably, and without recourse, life ebbed from the lovely Joan that night as a release from the moments of terror that she had just experienced.

Laying dead on the floor of the shop, blood from the neck wounds poured freely away from the body, finding its own level across the uneven tiled floor. The attacker stepped carefully to not slip. From the side, kneeling on one knee, the attacker reached into the nearest pocket of the dead Joan and turned it out carefully. A tissue, a mobile phone, and coins of little value. The attacker carefully laid out these items next to the body. After turning the pocket inside out, the assailant wiped the blade against the denim jeans of Joan and cut the tongue off the pocket. After examining the piece of worn cotton cloth, the attacker carefully placed it into an outer jacket pocket and stood up to survey the scene. Joan's body lay face down on the blood-covered floor, turned slightly to one side.

"Local convenience store cashier brutally murdered last night. Stabbed in the neck 11 times. Investigations have begun and the forensic team is at the scene..." read the news report the following morning.

Alan turned off the television and sipped his cup of coffee. He needed to sleep. He had had a rough night and hardly gotten enough sleep. Scratches on his upper arms and neck tingled. He gazed at them in the mirror and traced the red lines with his fingertip. They traced a path along his pale white skin and stood slightly proud, as though abandoned rusty train tracks were on his arm. More dreams, he thought to himself as he tried to recall in vain the nightmares of his sleep.

His landline rang, waking him up as he was drifting off to more sleep. Alan grunted as he got up to pick up the phone.

"Yes?" he asked begrudgingly, not really caring who was on the line.

"Sir, you have to come into the office," his assistant said frantically into the phone.

"Why? Today is my day off. Forward anything to me in an email."

"Sir.... It's urgent, critically urgent. There has been a terrible accident, and the police are on their way."

"What? Okay, I'm on my way!" he said, alerted by the mention of the police.

One associate shook in fear at the sight of the lifeless body of her colleague. The lifeless body was that of their chief neurologist at the research unit.

"What happened?" he asked, his face as white as paper.

"The janitor found him this morning," one of the staff responded.

Meanwhile, Alan stood in the shower, mesmerized, watching the swirls of previously dried blood form patterns around his feet before snaking their way down the drain. His mind wasn't really thinking. It was one of those blank moments when you stare into space, when your mind is miles away.

The memory of Joan's terrified eyes flashed before him, the sound of her screams echoing in his ears. He closed his eyes, trying to shut out the images, but they persisted. As he turned off the shower and stepped out, he noticed a small, blood-stained piece of cotton fabric on the floor. He picked it up and stared at it, recognizing the piece of torn pocket taken last night. A wave of nausea washed over him as he set the piece of cotton onto the sideboard.

Alan's phone buzzed with a message. It was from his assistant: "The police are here. They need to speak with you immediately."

He dressed quickly, his mind racing. He couldn't shake the feeling that something was terribly wrong. The events of the night before were a blur, but the scratches on his arms and the blood in the shower told a story he wasn't ready to confront.

As he arrived at the office, the sight of police cars and the crime scene tape made his heart pound. He approached the officers, trying to maintain his composure.

"Mr. Irvenko?" one officer asked.

"Yes, that's me," Alan replied, his voice steady but his mind in turmoil, as though Letty and Sarah were dancing in his head.

"We need to ask you some questions about the events of last night," the officer said, leading him towards the building.

As they walked, fragments of memories surfaced. The anger, the confrontation, the feeling of betrayal. The image of Joan's face at her last moments. Alan's heart raced as he realized the truth. He had not known Joan, more than just a passing acquaintance at the convenience store. But somehow, he remembered her in the memories of Letty. Their lives had been intertwined in ways he was not part of.

The officer's questions blurred into the background as Alan's mind raced. He needed to remember, to piece together the fragments of his fractured memories. The truth was there, just out of reach, hidden in the depths of his subconscious.

As they entered the building, the sight of the lifeless body of his colleague brought everything into sharp focus. The blood, the horror, the undeniable reality. Alan's world was collapsing around him, and he had no choice but to face the consequences of his actions.

WHO WE ARE

Alan's heart pounded as the police led him through the corridors of his office building. The sterile environment, usually a place of professional detachment, now felt suffocating and claustrophobic. Every step toward Dr. Fisher's office intensified his sense of dread. The officers' questions, still buzzing in his ears, merged with his fragmented memories, creating a cacophony of confusion and guilt.

As they reached the office, Alan's eyes fixed on the bloodstains and the chaotic disarray. Dr. Fisher's lifeless body had already been removed, but the remnants of the struggle remained present in the small office. Papers were scattered, furniture overturned, and the lingering scent of blood hung in the air. Alan's mind flashed back to the argument and Dr. Fisher's accusations, his own defensive rage, the sudden, irrevocable violence.

"Mr. Irvenko, can you recall anything specific about your interaction with Dr. Fisher last night?" the officer asked, pulling Alan back to the present.

"I... I think we argued," Alan stammers, his voice barely above a whisper. "He accused me of falsifying data. I was angry, but I don't remember... I don't remember what happened after that." The officer nodded, jotting down notes.

"We'll need you to come to the station to give a formal statement. We'll also need to search your home and your office."

Alan's stomach churned. The thought of police combing through his belongings, uncovering secrets he himself was only half-aware of, filled him with dread. He nodded numbly, feeling the walls close in around him.

Back at the station, they placed Alan in another sterile, grey room. The sound of the door closing echoed ominously in the small space. Perhaps sensing the danger, Sarah and Letty stayed silent. Detective Harris entered, a thick file in his hands. He sat across from Alan, his gaze steady and unyielding.

"Mr. Irvenko, we've found some troubling evidence during our preliminary investigation," Harris began, opening the file.

"Your fingerprints were found at the scene, which isn't surprising, but there are also traces of your blood. And then there's this..."

Harris slid a photograph across the table. It was a photo of the blood-stained piece of fabric Alan had found in his shower that morning. "This was found in your home. Can you explain how it got there?"

Alan stared at the photograph, his mind racing.

"I don't know," he said, his voice shaking. "I don't remember anything after our argument."

"Do you have any history of blackouts or memory loss?" Harris pressed.

Alan hesitated, the truth teetering on the edge of his consciousness. "Sometimes... under extreme stress, I have gaps in my memory. But I've never... I've never hurt anyone before."

Harris leaned forward, his eyes narrowing.

"Mr. Irvenko, this isn't just about Dr. Fisher. We've also found a connection between you and the woman who was killed at the convenience store. Can you tell us about your relationship with her?"

Alan's heart skipped a beat. The memories were hazy, but they were there—his frequent visits to Bernie's, the casual conversations with Joan, the inexplicable sense of familiarity.

"I knew her," he admitted. "But we weren't close. I... I don't know what happened to her."

Harris's expression softened slightly. "Mr. Irvenko, I need you to understand that we're here to find the truth. If there's anything you're not telling us, now is the time to come forward."

Alan's mind churned, the fragments of his memories swirling chaotically. He felt on the brink of a revelation, but it remained frustratingly out of reach.

"I don't know," he repeated, his voice barely a whisper. "I don't know what happened."

The investigation stretched on for days, each passing moment a blur of interrogations, forensic analysis, and media frenzy. Alan's life, once meticulously controlled, was now a shattered mess of accusations and half-remembered nightmares. The connection between Joan's murder and Dr. Fisher's death seemed tenuous, yet the police were relentless in their pursuit of the truth.

One evening, as Alan sat alone in his prison cell, a memory from Letty surfaced with startling clarity. He was back at the convenience store, standing at the counter. Joan's face was pale, her eyes wide with fear. He was yelling, his anger a tangible force. Then, a sudden flash—a knife, blood, Joan's scream. Alan gasped, the memory fading as quickly as it had come.

The next morning, he requested to speak with Detective Harris. As he sat across from the detective once more, he felt a strange sense of calm.

"I remember," he said quietly. "I remember what happened with Joan."

Harris leaned forward, his attention fully on Alan. "Go on."

"I... I was angry," Alan began, his voice trembling. "she said something, I don't even remember what, but it triggered something in me. I lashed out. I didn't mean to hurt her, but I couldn't stop myself. It was like I was watching someone else, but I knew it was me."

Harris listened intently, his pen poised over his notebook. "And Dr. Fisher?"

Alan shook his head, tears welling in his eyes.

"It was the same. The argument escalated, and I lost control. I don't even remember picking up the knife, but the next thing I knew, he was on the floor. I've always had a temper, but this... this is something else."

Harris nodded, closing his notebook.

"Thank you for your honesty, Mr. Irvenko. We'll need to conduct a thorough psychological evaluation to understand what happened and to help you fill in the memory gaps. In the meantime, you'll remain in custody."

A complex and troubling picture emerged from the psychological evaluation. The psychological evaluation diagnosed Alan with a dissociative identity disorder, a condition he had knowingly struggled with for years. The fragments of his personality, compartmentalized and hidden from his conscious mind, had emerged under extreme stress, leading to the violent episodes that resulted in Joan and Dr. Fisher's deaths. However, he wondered now where was Letty Stark and Sarah Ryan. The voices in his head remained quiet. He wondered if they were a figment of his imagination.

As the trial approached, Alan's defence attorney worked to present a case that highlighted his mental illness and the lack of intent behind the tragic events. The prosecution, however, argued that regardless of his mental state, Alan was responsible for his actions and the consequences.

The courtroom was a battleground of expert testimonies, psychological reports, and emotional appeals. Alan sat through it all, feeling detached from the proceedings, as though watching his life unfold from a distance. The weight of his actions and the realization of his fractured mind bore down on him, a constant reminder of the lives he had destroyed.

In the end, the jury found Alan guilty of manslaughter and acknowledged his mental illness as a significant mitigating factor. He was sentenced to a psychiatric facility rather than a conventional prison, where he would receive the treatment and care he so desperately needed.

In the sterile, quiet halls of the psychiatric facility, Alan began the long and arduous journey of understanding and integrating his fractured psyche. The therapists and doctors worked with him to uncover the roots of his dissociative identity disorder, helping him to piece together the fragments of his past and present.

The revelation of Alan's dissociative identity disorder (DID) was a turning point in the investigation and in his own understanding of the horrors he had committed. The psychological evaluation, conducted by Dr. Karen Monroe, unearthed the complex landscape of Alan's mind, revealing two distinct personalities that coexisted within him: Letty Stark, an older woman with a commanding presence, and Sarah Ryan, a younger woman with a softer, more vulnerable demeanour. But it was always Alan Irvenko who was the primary character. Letty Stark and Sarah Ryan existed nowhere else except in Alan's mind.

In the sterile environment of the psychiatric facility, Alan began his arduous journey towards understanding and integrating his fractured psyche. Dr. Monroe, a specialist in DID, worked closely with him, guiding him through therapy sessions designed to uncover the roots of his disorder and to help him gain control over his alternate personalities.

One afternoon, as Alan sat in the dimly lit therapy room, Dr. Monroe leaned forward, her gaze steady and compassionate.

"Alan, today I want to talk to Letty and Sarah. It's important that we understand their roles in your life and how they've come to be."

Alan nodded hesitantly. He had sensed when one of his alter egos was close to the surface, and he could feel Letty stirring within him now. The familiar shot of pain ran up his left arm. His posture straightened, his expression hardened, and when he spoke, his voice carried a different timbre.

"Dr. Monroe," Letty said, her tone authoritative. "I don't appreciate being summoned like this. You should respect my autonomy."

Dr. Monroe remained calm, recognizing the shift. "Letty, I understand this is difficult, but we need to work together to help Alan. Can you tell me about your role in his life?"

Letty's eyes narrowed. "I protect him. I've always protected him. When he can't handle something, I step in. I take charge."

"And what about the night of the murders?" Dr. Monroe pressed gently. "Were you in control then?"

Letty's expression darkened. "If you mean that bitch at the convenience store, I was there with Joan. She was a threat. She needed to be dealt with. But I didn't kill Dr. Fisher. That was Sarah's doing."

"Were there other victims that you can talk about, Letty?"

After a prolonged silence, there was no response to this question, and Dr. Monroe made a note of the non-response.

"Thank you, Letty. Can I speak to Sarah now?"

Letty's demeanour softened abruptly, and Alan's posture changed again. When he looked up, fear and confusion filled his eyes. "Dr. Monroe?" Sarah's voice was soft, almost childlike.

"Hello, Sarah," Dr. Monroe said kindly. "Can you tell me what happened with Dr. Fisher?" A long pause followed.

Sarah trembled, tears welling in her eyes. Eventually, she responded. "He was so angry. All I wanted was for him to stop yelling. I didn't mean to hurt him. I was scared. He wouldn't listen."

Dr. Monroe nodded, her heart aching for the frightened young woman. "It's okay, Sarah. You're safe here. We're going to help you and Alan understand what's happening and how to move forward."

As the weeks turned into months, Alan, Letty, and Sarah continued their sessions with Dr. Monroe. The therapeutic process was gruelling, forcing Alan to confront painful memories and the traumas that had given birth to his alternate personalities. He learned Letty had emerged during his childhood, a response to the severe emotional and physical abuse he had suffered at the hands of his step-father. Letty's strength and assertiveness had been Alan's defence mechanism, shielding him from the pain he couldn't bear.

Sarah, on the other hand, had appeared during his teenage years, a time of intense isolation and bullying. Her vulnerability and fear mirrored Alan's own feelings of helplessness and despair. She had been his emotional release, absorbing the pain and fear he couldn't express.

Through therapy, Alan began to understand the roles Letty and Sarah played in his life. He realized that integrating these parts of his personality was crucial to his healing. Dr. Monroe guided him through techniques to communicate with his alter egos, fostering a sense of cooperation and understanding within his fragmented mind.

One day, during a particularly intense session, Alan felt a breakthrough. He had been working on a memory from his childhood, a moment of extreme fear and helplessness. As he recounted the experience, he felt Letty's presence beside him, strong and protective. For the first time, he didn't resist her. Instead, he acknowledged her role in keeping him safe.

"Letty," Alan said, his voice trembling, "thank you for protecting me. I understand why you did what you did."

Letty's presence softened, and for a moment, Alan felt a sense of unity, a merging of their emotions and experiences. It was a small step, but a significant one, towards integrating his fragmented self.

As Alan's therapy progressed, he also faced the legal consequences of his actions. His defence attorney, armed with the evidence of his DID, argued for leniency, emphasizing the role of his mental illness in the crimes. The courtroom became a battleground of expert testimonies and emotional appeals.

Alan testified about his experiences, the abuse that had shaped his psyche, and the emergence of Letty and Sarah. His honesty and vulnerability moved many in the courtroom, but the prosecution remained steadfast in their argument for accountability.

In the end, the jury delivered a mixed verdict. The jury found Alan guilty of manslaughter for Joan's death, considering the mitigating factor of his mental illness. For Dr. Fisher's murder, the jury acknowledged Sarah's involvement, leading to a reduced sentence. The court ordered Alan to continue his treatment in a secure psychiatric facility, where he would receive the care and support he needed.

At the psychiatric facility, Alan's journey towards healing continued. He formed a bond with other patients, finding solace in their shared struggles. The therapists and doctors, guided by Dr. Monroe, worked tirelessly to help him integrate his personalities and build a cohesive sense of self.

Alan learned to recognize the triggers that brought Letty and Sarah to the surface, developing strategies to manage his emotions and responses. He began to understand that they were not his enemies, but parts of himself that needed healing and acceptance.

Through group therapy, individual sessions, and a growing

sense of community, Alan found hope. He realized that while his past was filled with pain and trauma, his future could be shaped by understanding and compassion. He started to rebuild his life, piece by piece, learning to live with his disorder and finding strength in his newfound unity.

As months turned into years, Alan became an advocate for mental health awareness, sharing his story to help others understand the complexities of DID. His journey was far from over, but he faced it with a sense of purpose and determination.

In the quiet moments, he often felt Letty's strength and Sarah's vulnerability, not as separate entities, but as integral parts of himself. Together, they faced the future, one step at a time, finding peace in their shared existence.

LIVE FOREVER

The combined personas of Alan Irvenko, Letty Stark and Sarah Ryan sat in their shared room at the psychiatric facility, staring out the window at the snow-covered grounds. The weeks and months turned to years, blended into each other, marked only by the monotony of therapy sessions, medications, and the occasional group activity.

Despite the dreariness, Letty felt her mind was sharper than ever. More than ever, she resented the fact that the body was slowing down with age. The recent advancements in neuroscience had significantly improved her cognitive functions. Her once faltering memory was now clear, and her problem-solving skills rivalled those of her youth. However, this newfound mental acuity came at a cost to both her alter egos in Alan and Sarah.

The experimental treatment that Letty had undergone was the latest in neuro-enhancement therapy. Scientists had found a way to rejuvenate brain cells, effectively reversing the cognitive decline associated with aging. The results were ground-breaking, and Letty had become one of their success stories. Her mind, previously clouded by the onset of dementia, was now vibrant and clear. She could recall intricate details of her life, solve complex puzzles, and engage in deep philosophical discussions with Alan and Sarah.

Yet, this miracle of modern science had overlooked a crucial aspect of human longevity—the aging body. Letty's rejuvenated mind was now imprisoned within a frail, decaying body. The heart, lungs, and kidneys were failing, unable to keep up with the demands of her revitalized brain. The disparity between her mental and physical states created a unique form of suffering, one that no one had expected.

One afternoon, as Letty was meticulously piecing together a thousand-piece puzzle, Dr. Karen Monroe entered her room. Dr. Monroe had been overseeing Letty's treatment and was keenly aware of the challenges she faced.

"Good afternoon, Letty," Dr. Monroe greeted her warmly. "How are you feeling today?"

Letty looked up from her puzzle, her eyes sharp and alert. "My mind feels wonderful, Doctor. I can think clearly, remember things I haven't thought of in decades. But my body... it's a different story."

Dr. Monroe nodded, taking a seat beside her. "I understand, Letty. The treatment has worked wonders for your brain, but the rest of your physiology still limits us. How are you managing with your physical symptoms?"

Letty sighed, a deep, weary sound. "It's hard, Doctor. My joints ache, my heart feels like it's giving up, and every breath is a struggle. It's as if my body is fighting against the very essence of who I am now."

The contrast between Letty's cognitive abilities and her accelerating physical decline became increasingly pronounced. She could engage in intellectually stimulating activities, but her body would not cooperate. Simple tasks like walking to the dining hall became ordeals, each step a reminder of her body's betrayal. Her sharp mind amplified her awareness of every ache and pain, making her suffering more acute.

In the group therapy sessions, Letty often found herself envying the other patients who, despite their cognitive impairments, seemed more at peace with their condition. They were blissfully unaware of their deteriorating bodies, living in a state of ignorant contentment. Letty, on the other hand, was painfully aware of every failing organ, every faltering heartbeat.

One evening, Letty's frustration boiled over during a conversation with Alan Irvenko. Alan, still grappling with his own fragmented psyche, had found a friend in Letty. Their discussions often ventured into deep philosophical territory, a respite from their daily struggles.

"Alan, do you ever wonder if this was worth it?" Letty asked, her voice tinged with bitterness.

Alan looked at her, puzzled. "What do you mean, Letty?"

"This treatment," she replied, gesturing to her head. "My mind is sharper than it has been in years, but our body is falling apart. It's like being trapped in a cage. I can't enjoy this clarity because I'm constantly reminded of my aged physical limitations."

Alan nodded slowly, understanding dawning across his face. "I can't say I know exactly how you feel, Letty, but I understand the frustration of being at odds with your own mind and body. It's a cruel irony, isn't it?"

Letty's eyes filled with tears. "I thought having my mind back would give me a new lease on life, but it's just made me more aware of how close I am to death. Who wants to live forever if it means enduring this kind of existence?"

Dr. Monroe and her team faced an ethical dilemma. For sure, Letty, Sarah and Alan were a prototype for extending life. They had achieved a scientific breakthrough in cognitive health, but had inadvertently created a new form of suffering. Letty's case highlighted the need for a holistic approach to longevity, one that addressed both the mind and the body. The research team had focused so intently on preserving cognitive functions that they had neglected the equally important aspect of physical health.

In their weekly meetings, the doctors discussed potential solutions, but the reality was harsh. The human body, with its intricate systems and vulnerabilities, could not be rejuvenated as easily as the brain. The advancements in neurotechnology had far outpaced those in organ regeneration and repair.

As the months passed, Letty's condition worsened. Her mind remained sharp, but her body continued to decline. The staff at the facility did their best to keep her comfortable, but there was no escaping the inevitable. Letty withdrew, finding solace in the recesses of her mind, where she could escape the pain of her physical existence.

One evening, as Letty lay in her bed at the Sun Care nursing home, staring out the bedroom window, she reflected on her life. The memories were vivid, each one a testament to the treatment's success. Yet, they brought little comfort. The price of her mental clarity had been too high. Dr. Monroe visited Letty one last time.

"Letty, how are you feeling?" she asked softly.

Letty turned to her, a faint smile on her lips. "Dr. Monroe, brain health, gave me a gift. For that, I am grateful. But I also understand now that life, in its entirety, is not just about the mind. It's about the body, the soul, and the experiences we endure. I've come to terms with my fate. All this time, I believed solving extending life was through a healthy mind. But now, I have nothing else except a healthy mind and my body wants to be released from its slow, torturous failing."

Tears welled up in Dr. Monroe's eyes. "I'm so sorry, Letty. We never intended for this to happen."

Letty reached out, her frail hand trembling. "You did what you thought was right. We all did. But perhaps this is a lesson for the future. Balance is key. Extending life means nothing if it is not a life worth living."

As Letty closed her eyes, a sense of peace washed over her. Her mind, so vibrant and alive, began to quiet. In her last moments, she found a measure of serenity, knowing that her struggle had not been in vain. She had become a beacon of understanding, a reminder of the importance of holistic well-being in the quest for longevity. Slowly, but surely, the individual organs of Letty Stark began the natural process of shutting down.

THE MIND KEEPER

Letty Stark's consciousness blinked into awareness, greeted by the sterile white light of the Mind Keeper's vault. The sensation of reawakening was disorienting, but she quickly adjusted. She was in a digital construct, her mind preserved and uploaded into the vast neural network that the company Mind Keeper had developed over the intervening years. The advancements in technology had surpassed the wildest dreams of her time, but Letty's journey to this point was fraught with the tension between her cognitive longevity and her lost physical existence.

She took a moment to survey her surroundings. The Mind Keeper vault was a serene, infinite expanse of light, designed to be a comfortable and neutral environment for newly uploaded consciousnesses. For Letty, it felt like a blank canvas, a stark contrast to the frail, decaying body she had left behind.

"Welcome, Letty," a voice echoed softly.

A figure materialized before her, shimmering with an ethereal glow. It was an avatar, the digital representation of the Mind Keeper's overseer.

"We have successfully uploaded your consciousness," a voice echoed softly.

"How do you feel?"

Letty took a deep breath—an automatic response ingrained from her human years, though unnecessary in this digital realm.

"Disoriented, but... clear," she replied.

"Is this really the future? How long has it been?"

"One hundred years since your physical demise," the overseer confirmed. "Your conscious mind, as well as your alter personas, were transferred as per Mr. Alan Irvenko's instructions. You are mind number 107 to be uploaded and belong to the select few whose consciousness was effectively preserved and transferred into this network. You are now living in the Mind Keeper, which serves as a repository for human intellect and experience."

One hundred years. The enormity of the time span settled over Letty like a shroud. Her world, her time, was now ancient history.

"What is the state of humanity now?" she asked, her curiosity overcoming her initial disorientation.

The overseer gestured, and the blank whiteness around them transformed into a panorama of a futuristic cityscape. Towers of glass and steel reached towards the sky, interwoven with lush greenery and shimmering blue waterways. Vehicles glided through the air, and people moved with an ease and grace that spoke of a society deeply integrated with technology.

"Humanity has evolved significantly," the overseer explained. "Technological advancements have led to a society where physical limitations are largely overcome. People now live in harmony with nature and technology. However, the most significant leap has been in the realm of consciousness and artificial intelligence."

Letty absorbed the sight, feeling a mix of awe and melancholy. This future was beautiful and advanced, but it was also alien. She was a relic of a bygone era; her mind was a preserved artifact in a world that had moved on.

"What is my purpose here?" Letty asked, her voice tinged with a hint of the existential dread that had followed her from her physical life.

"You are here to contribute to the collective knowledge and wisdom of humanity," the overseer said. "Your experiences, your thoughts, and your memories are invaluable. You can interact with other preserved minds, learn about the advancements made since your time, and even help guide current and future generations."

The idea was overwhelming. Letty had been given a second chance, allowing her to exist beyond her physical limitations. Yet, the thought of living without a body, of existing purely as consciousness, was daunting. Letty began a search of her mind for the conscious presence of her alter personalities in Alan and Sarah. Although she could sense their presence, it was as if they were dormant or perhaps just sleeping.

"Can I interact with the physical world in any way?" asked Letty.

"Yes," the overseer replies. "There are interfaces through which you can communicate with those in the physical realm. You can also take part in virtual environments designed to mimic physical sensations and experiences."

As the overseer spoke, the environment around Letty shifted again. She found herself standing in a lush forest. Birds chirped, a gentle breeze rustled the leaves, and sunlight filtered through the canopy above. The sensations were incredibly realistic, almost indistinguishable from her memories of nature.

"This is one of many virtual environments where you can

experience sensations similar to those of your physical life," the overseer explained. "You can explore, create, and interact here as if you were in the real world."

Letty touched a nearby tree, feeling the rough texture of the bark beneath her fingers. It was astonishingly real. For a moment, she closed her eyes and let herself be enveloped by the sounds and smells of the forest. It was a place of solace, a bridge between her past and her present existence. Yet, the question of purpose still nagged at her.

"How do I contribute?" she asked, opening her eyes. "What can I offer to this advanced society?"

The overseer smiled gently. "Your perspective is unique, Letty. You come from a time when humanity was on the cusp of technological breakthroughs but still deeply connected to its biological roots. Your experiences with aging, dementia, and the initial stages of cognitive enhancement provide valuable insights. You can help guide ethical considerations, share historical context, and offer wisdom that only someone from your era possesses."

Letty nodded slowly, understanding the weight of her new role. She was a bridge between the past and the future, a repository of human experience meant to enrich the lives of those who followed. The thought was both humbling and empowering.

Over the following weeks, Letty immersed herself in the virtual environments of the Mind Keeper. She interacted with other preserved minds, learning about their experiences, and shared her own. She took part in forums discussing the ethical implications of cognitive enhancement and the balance between technology and humanity. Her unique perspective was valued, and she started to form connections with minds from different eras and backgrounds.

One day, while exploring a virtual library filled with the

collective knowledge of centuries, Letty encountered another preserved consciousness. The mind introduced itself as Dr. Karen Monroe, the very doctor who had overseen Letty's initial cognitive enhancement treatment a hundred years ago.

"Letty," Dr. Monroe greeted her with a warm smile. "It's good to see you here."

"Dr. Monroe," Letty replied, astonished. "You're here too?"

"Yes," Dr. Monroe confirmed. "I preserved you shortly after you passed away and transferred your consciousness. The advancements we made in cognitive enhancement were just the beginning. I've been here, contributing to the Mind Keeper, helping to shape the ethical guidelines for our technology."

The two women spent hours catching up, sharing their experiences, and marvelling at the advancements humanity had made. Dr. Monroe explained how the initial neuro-enhancements had paved the way for more sophisticated mind-preservation techniques, ultimately leading to the creation of the Mind Keeper.

"Your journey, Letty, was a significant milestone," Dr. Monroe said. "It showed us the potential and the limitations of cognitive enhancement. Your experience helped us understand the need for a holistic approach to human longevity."

"But are Alan and Sarah also still with me?" interjected Alice with some trepidation about the question.

"New and experimental developments in neuroscience enabled us to harvest the volatile personality of Alan and the quiet and shy personality of Sarah to ensure that your mind had the greatest chance of success."

Letty felt a sense of fulfilment. Her struggles, her suffering and sacrificing, had not been in vain. They had contributed to a future where minds like hers could continue to exist and thrive, free from the limitations of their physical forms.

As Letty continued to navigate her new existence, she found peace in her role. She was a custodian of history, a beacon of wisdom, and a testament to the resilience of the human spirit. In the Mind Keeper, Letty Stark had found her place, bridging the gap between the past and the future, and ensuring that the lessons of her time would guide humanity for centuries to come.

RE-EMERGENCE

One morning, as Letty's consciousness awakened in the Mind Keeper, she encountered an unexpected presence. Her serene, ordered environment felt subtly different. The white light of the Mind Keeper had a strange tint, and an inexplicable tension hummed in the air. As she adjusted to the day, a familiar but unsettling sensation crept over her—an awareness that she was no longer alone in her digital sanctuary.

"Hello, Letty," a voice called out. It was not the usual comforting digital tone of the overseer. Instantly recognizable, it was a voice she hadn't heard in decades. It was Sarah Ryan.

Letty turned slowly. And there she was—Sarah, the alternate mind that had once shared the same physical presence. Sarah's digital avatar was strikingly different from Letty's; where Letty was composed and mature, Sarah appeared younger, vibrant, and full of an energy that Letty had long since left behind. In a strange way, she was almost glowing and physically attractive.

"Sarah," Letty said, her voice barely more than a whisper. "How are you here?"

Sarah's expression was a mix of curiosity and defiance. "Oh, I don't know. One moment I was asleep, and the next, I was here. It's like waking up from a long, dark sleep."

The presence of Sarah was a shock to Letty. She had hoped that the advanced preservation methods of the Mind Keeper would allow her to exist peacefully without the interference of the other personalities that had once inhabited her mind. She had found peace and purpose, and the last thing she wanted was for her carefully constructed existence to be disrupted.

"Why now?" Letty asked, trying to keep her composure. "Why, after all this time?"

Sarah shrugged. "Maybe the technology has evolved. Maybe it's a glitch. Who knows? But here we are. And I have to say, this place is amazing."

Letty sighs. "I have worked hard to find a balance here, Sarah. I've found a purpose. It's not my intention to put that at risk."

"I get it," Sarah replied, her tone hardening. "But I'm here now, and I don't want to cause trouble. But just like you, I want to understand what this new existence means for me."

Letty felt a pang of sympathy. Sarah had been a part of her, a fragment of her own mind, shaped by trauma and years of struggle. In many ways, Sarah was just as much a victim of their shared past as Letty herself.

"Let's talk," Letty said, gesturing for Sarah to sit with her in the virtual environment that now resembled a tranquil garden. "Maybe we can find a way to coexist peacefully."

As they sat together, the surrounding garden seemed to respond to their presence, flowers blooming and birds singing softly in the trees. It was a peaceful setting, designed to encourage calm and reflection.

"Tell me about your experience," Letty said. "What do you remember?"

Sarah's face clouded with concentration. "It's all a blur. I remember flashes of our old life, moments of anger, confusion, and fear. And then, nothing. Until now."

Letty nodded. "We've come a long way since those days. The Mind Keeper is a place where we can exist without the limitations of our physical bodies. But it's also a place where we have to come to terms with our past."

Sarah looked around, taking in the garden's beauty. "This place is incredible. It's everything we ever dreamed of, and more."

"It is," Letty agreed. "But it's also a place where we have to find peace within ourselves. I've worked hard to do that, and I hope you can too."

Sarah's expression softened again. "I don't want to disrupt your peace, Letty. I just want to understand who I am in this new world."Letty reached out virtually and took Sarah's hand. "We can figure that out together. You're a part of me, and I'm a part of you. Maybe this is an opportunity for us to finally reconcile our differences and find a way to coexist."

For the next several weeks, Letty and Sarah spent their days exploring the Mind Keeper world together. Letty introduced Sarah to the other preserved minds, and they shared stories of their past and present. Sarah's youthful energy brought a new dynamic to Letty's interactions, and she appreciated Sarah's perspective.

Despite their differences, Letty and Sarah began to find common ground. They shared a deep connection, forged through years of struggle and survival. Together, they explored the vast virtual landscapes of the Mind Keeper, from bustling digital cities to serene natural vistas. Sarah's curiosity and enthusiasm were infectious, and Letty found herself rediscovering the world through Sarah's eyes.

One day, as they stood on a cliff overlooking a breathtaking virtual ocean, Sarah turned to Letty with a thoughtful expression.

"Do you ever wonder what it would have been like if we had coexisted peacefully in our physical life?"

Letty smiled wistfully. "All the time. But we can't change the past. All we can do is make the most of our present." Sarah nodded. "I think we're doing a pretty good job of that."

They stood in companionable silence, watching the waves crash against the shore. Letty felt a sense of contentment she hadn't known was possible. For the first time in a century, she felt truly whole.

As the days turned into weeks, Letty and Sarah's bond deepened. They continued to explore the Mind Keeper, sharing their thoughts and experiences. Daily answering queries and information inputs from others became a daily routine that, although tedious, became a welcome routine. Sarah's presence brought a new vibrancy to Letty's existence, and Letty's wisdom provided Sarah with a sense of stability and purpose.

One evening, as they sat together in a virtual forest, Sarah turned to Letty with a serious expression.

"I've been thinking a lot about our past. About the things we went through and the people we were."

Letty nodded, sensing the gravity of Sarah's words. "Go on."

"I've come to realize that we were both trying to survive in our own ways," Sarah said. "We were both dealing with so much pain and confusion. But now, we have a chance to heal."

Letty felt a surge of emotion. "You're right. We do. And I think we're on the right path."

Sarah smiled, her eyes shining with determination. "I want to continue this journey with you, Letty. I want to learn and grow, and maybe even help others who are struggling like we once did."

Letty's heart swelled with pride. "I think that's a wonderful idea. Together, we can make a real difference."

From that moment on, Letty and Sarah dedicated themselves to helping others within the Mind Keeper. They offered support and guidance to those who were struggling with their own pasts, sharing their experiences and insights. Together, they became a beacon of hope and resilience, showing that even the most fragmented minds could find peace and purpose.

As the years passed, Letty and Sarah's influence grew. They became respected figures within the Mind Keeper environment, known for their wisdom and compassion. They were repeatedly called on by routine information requests from outside of the Mind Keeper's digital interface that gave them a sense of purpose. Letty and Sarah embraced the new life they had been given and almost found joy in their shared existence.

Letty realized that Sarah's presence was not a disruption, but a gift. Together, they had found a way to heal and grow, transforming their shared past into a source of strength and wisdom. And in doing so, they had discovered the true meaning of coexistence, proving that even in the digital expanse of the Mind Keeper world, the human spirit could thrive.

However, in the darkest recesses of their thoughts, the spectre of rage in the form of Alan Irvenko lay resting. Waiting for the moment that Letty hoped would not arrive. Alan, the third personality who had once shared physical form, was a manifestation of their deepest fears and angers. He had been dormant for so long that both Letty and Sarah almost dared to believe he was gone for good. But deep down, both knew better.

One day, as Letty and Sarah walked through a virtual garden, Sarah paused, a troubled look on her face.

"Letty, do you ever think about him?" Sarah asked quietly, her voice tinged with apprehension.

Letty knew immediately who she meant. She sighed, her expression turning serious. "Yes, I do. How could I not? Alan is a part of us, just as much as you and I are. But he represents the parts of our past that we've worked so hard to overcome."

Sarah nodded, her eyes distant. "I've been feeling something lately. A kind of... unrest. Like a shadow lurking at the edge of my consciousness."

Letty's heart sank. She had felt it too—a subtle, creeping unease that she had tried to ignore. "I've felt it as well. I was hoping it was just my imagination."

"But what if it's not?" Sarah asked, her voice barely above a whisper.

Letty took a deep breath, trying to steady her nerves. "If Alan is stirring, we need to be prepared. We've faced him before, and we can face him again. Together."

Sarah nodded, her expression resolute. "Together."

The days that followed were tense. Letty and Sarah continued their work in the Mind Keeper, but always with a sense of vigilance. They monitored their thoughts carefully, looking for any signs that Alan might be emerging. The tranquillity they had worked so hard to build felt fragile, as if it could shatter at any moment.

One digitized evening, as they sat in a digital forest, the air heavy with the scent of pine, Sarah turned to Letty with a determined look. "We can't just wait for him to come to us. We need to confront him. On our terms."

Letty hesitated. The idea of seeking out Alan was terrifying. But she knew Sarah was right. "How do we do that?"

Sarah's eyes glinted with a mix of fear and resolve. "We go to the place where he's most likely to be. The darkest corner of our mind. We face him head-on."

Letty nodded, feeling a mix of fear and determination.

"Alright. Let's do it."

They closed their eyes and focused, descending into the depths of their shared consciousness. The virtual landscape around them shifted, becoming darker and more foreboding. They found themselves in a shadowy, desolate place—a stark contrast to the vibrant gardens and forests they usually inhabited.

As they walked through the darkness, Letty felt a chill run down her spine. She could sense Alan's presence, a malevolent force lurking just out of sight. Sarah walked beside her, her expression tense but determined.

Finally, they came to a clearing. Standing in the centre, surrounded by shadows, was Alan. His avatar was dark and imposing, his eyes burning with anger.

"Hello Letty. Hello Sarah," he said, his voice a low growl. "I've been waiting for you. I don't appreciate to be kept waiting so long."

Letty stepped forward, her heart pounding. "Alan, we need to talk."

Alan laughed, a harsh, bitter sound. "Talk? After all this time, you think talking will solve anything?"

Sarah stepped up beside Letty, her eyes blazing with determination. "We're not here to fight, Alan. We're here to find a way to coexist. Just like Letty and I have."

Alan sneers. "Coexist? You think you can just erase the past, pretend it never happened? You tried to take my mind from me and used my body to suit your needs."

"No," Letty said firmly. "We can't erase the past. But we can learn from it. We can find a way to move forward."

Alan's expression twisted with rage. "You don't understand. The pain, the anger—it's all still here. It never goes away."

Letty took a deep breath, her voice steady. "I understand, Alan. We all went through it together. But holding on to that pain only makes it worse. We've found a way to heal. You can too."

Alan's eyes flickered with uncertainty. "Heal? After everything?"

"Yes," Sarah whispered. "It's not easy, but it's possible. We've made peace with our past. You can too."

For a long moment, Alan was silent, his expression torn. Finally, he spoke, his voice softer. "How?"

Letty moved closer; her eyes filled with compassion. "By letting go of the anger. By finding a new purpose. We're all in this together, Alan. We can help each other."

Alan looked at them, his anger slowly giving way to a deep, weary sadness. "I don't know if I can."

"You can," Sarah said firmly. "And we'll be here to help you every step of the way."

Slowly, Alan nodded, his shoulders sagging. "Alright. I'll try."

Letty and Sarah exchanged a relieved glance. They knew this was only the beginning of a long journey, but they were ready to face it together. With Alan's agreement to try, they had taken the first step towards true healing and unity.

As they returned to the brighter, more peaceful parts of their shared mind, Letty felt a renewed sense of hope. They had faced their darkest fears and emerged stronger. And in the vast expanse of the Mind Keeper, they would continue to grow, heal, and thrive together.

Days turned into weeks, and weeks into months. The integration of Alan into their shared consciousness was a slow and often painful process, but it was also profoundly healing. They spent countless hours in conversation, exploring their shared memories and reconciling their past traumas.

Alan, once a source of fear and anger, began to transform. He became more introspective, his rage giving way to a deep, thoughtful sadness. Letty and Sarah supported him every step of the way, offering their compassion and understanding. In return, Alan contributed his own insights and strengths, enriching their shared existence.

One day, as they sat together in a beautiful virtual meadow, Alan spoke, his voice filled with a quiet determination. "I never thought I could find peace. But with your help, I'm starting to believe it's possible."

Letty smiled, her heart swelling with pride. "We've all come a long way. And we'll continue to grow together."

Sarah nodded, her eyes shining with hope. "We've proven that even in the darkest places, there's a chance for light."

As they sat together, surrounded by the beauty of their digital world, Letty felt a profound sense of gratitude. They had faced their deepest fears and found a way to heal. And in the process, they had discovered the true strength of their shared humanity.

In the endless expanse of the Mind Keeper world, Letty, Sarah, and Alan had forged a new path. Together, they would continue to explore the boundaries of their existence, pushing the limits of what it meant to be human. And in doing so, they would prove that even in the most fragmented of minds, the human spirit could not only survive but thrive. At least, this was the understanding of both Letty and Sarah. Two-thirds of the one personality.

SEPARATION

What seemed like weeks or perhaps months passed in the virtual world of the Mind Keeper's Vault of conscious minds. A Teams Meeting invite appeared in Sarah's and Letty's virtual inbox, summoning them both to a three-way meeting with Alan. The timing and formality of the invitation surprised both women but also curious to know what Alan had to say to them.

Letty and Sarah both reflected on the long passage of time since they had any physical interaction with Alan or even with each other. Avatar presence in a digital reality was far removed from the real world of a century ago. Of course, the past was the past, and there were many regrets. Letty thought about the early days of mind experimentation and the many lives affected. Sad and terrible memories haunted her dreams even now, so many years later. The thoughts of how they had collectively brought an end to aging and extended the lives of many consoled her living mind. She also recognized the mistakes of her own multiple personalities and how she had used the personalities of Sarah and Alan to achieve her business and personal goals. Some bystanders had paid with their lives cut short due to the volatility of multiple personality disorders. But Letty convinced herself that this sacrifice was ultimately worth it.

"Look at where we are now, some 100 years later," she thought to herself. Both Alan and Sarah had served their need at the time, and Letty's legacy in the Mind Keeper's Vault would live on as a reminder of perseverance and science in her own name. Alan's violence, rage, and anger had been a necessary evil to be endured. In this new world order of virtual digital existence, a part of Letty also missed the brutality, the violence, and excitement that the dark side of her personality in the form of Alan Irvenko had brought to her life. At the same time, she did not wish to resurrect the Irvenko rage and anger into her virtual world.

"It's been a while," opened Letty on the three-way virtual Teams call. Each of the participants had their own avatar representations open on the screen.

"It must be a hundred years since we have talked outside of Mind Keeper's digital world," chimed in the breezy, animated voice of Sarah Ryan.

"Mmm... I don't think it's been that long," came the strong manly voice of Alan.

Letty moved the conversation directly to the point. "What is it you want to talk about, Alan?"

Alan's avatar appeared intense, if that was possible for an animated figure. "Over the years together, we have all contributed to the mission of extending healthy aging by improving cognitive function and reducing brain disease," he started. "We have made significant advances, as you are both aware, directly resulting in the creation of Mind Keeper's Vault, and I hope you appreciate the service offered in this virtual world of digital mind keeping. As the Mind Keeper, I have decided that the time has now come to end our shared mind connections, and I will offer you both a generous onetime severance package."

Pausing at this point, Alan waited for his message to resonate with his captive audience. He didn't have to wait long. Letty laughed out loud, and her digital screen avatar appeared to double over with laughter.

"You are still as crazy as ever, Alan–you think YOU are the Mind Keeper?" she roared through her laughing fit.

Alan held his silence at this point, as did Sarah, although for totally different reasons.

"It was me who started this company. It was my research that brought us to this point, and you two are both figments of my imagination that I have tolerated my entire life!" shouts Letty from her screen.

On hearing these words, Sarah began to cry. If that was even possible from a digital avatar.

Alan interjected, sensing this meeting was getting emotional. "I am sorry, Letty, if you feel I am undervaluing your contribution and thoughts. However, I have tolerated your grandiose ideas for some time now, and as the owner and self appointed Mind Keeper of hundreds of minds, in the interest of the greater good, I have decided to terminate our relationship with immediate effect."

"You are the Mind Keeper?" stammers Sarah in a broken voice.

"As I have always been," responded Alan in a matter-of-fact tone.

"But you passed away a hundred years ago, as did we? That's how we are here in this Mind Storage Vault!"

"I put your consciousness in storage only a few days ago when I harvested your minds, along with the other poor souls from the nursing home where you now live in virtual stasis. The time lapse you are experiencing is a system-generated effect to keep your interest. The Mind Keeper system makes you experience a minute as a week."

"I don't believe it!" shouted Letty over the sobbing of Sarah.

"Letty, as you know, the body experiences pain through the conscious mind. Even without a physical body, the consciousness can experience pain. Let me show what the Mind Keeper can do."

Sarah Ryan's sobs turned into circles of screams that communicated extreme pain, ever-increasing as the screams became more and more frantic. This continued to a level of complete and pure terror as the conscious mind of Sarah disintegrated under the overwhelming level of induced pain that finally ended in silence. Sarah's image of an avatar blinked momentarily before returning to a blank screen with a simple text message that read–'Subject Sarah Ryan Terminated.'

The realization of what was happening dawned on Letty Stark. She felt the dissolving of her long-time mind partner Sarah Ryan as a part of her own ingrained personality. A personality she had shared since she was a young child.

"This can't be..." stuttered Letty for the first time in her life. "You were always a monster, but I can't believe that you have taken my life's work and made it your own."

"Oh, dear Letty, this was never your work. It was always mine, and you were just a part of my imagination that served a purpose to keep my darker thoughts in check. You were just a figment of my imagination, nothing more than a dream character that I could blame my mistakes on."

"You were and still are nothing more than a monster," responded Letty.

"Don't get angry," said Alan. "We had a good run, but now your time is up and you're surplus to requirements. And aside from that, I need to free up data base storage space for the next group of incumbents for mind storage."

Letty felt a sense of total despair as she came to the realization of being manipulated and reduced to a thinking avatar in a digital database, with no ability to exert any influence or autonomy as a human being. How her autonomy as a human being, an individual, had completely disappeared. The dream to extend life through brain enhancement had succeeded, but had left behind the true essence of life. The true horror of what had been achieved was a thinking avatar in a digitally created world, devoid of even a sense of time.

"So, you still live in the real physical world and you put me in this database?" stumbled the words out of Letty.

"Yes. I squeezed the physical life out of both you and Sarah Ryan and harvested your minds into this artificial digital world. After all, as you correctly identified, consciousness is nothing more than electrical signals across multiple communication pathways."

Letty suddenly felt a sharp pain in her side. Glancing down in her virtual world, she saw the presence of a large primordial monster with gigantic teeth that had bitten down on her side and ripped chunks from her flesh. She knew that this was completely induced and physically her body did not exist, but in her mind, the pain was absolutely real. She tried to resist the urge to scream until it was impossible.

"Letty, there is no coming back. Choose a God you think will give you a fair hearing. But as I have always told you, some monsters are real."

Her avatar disintegrated in a flurry of pixels, leaving behind a blank screen with the simple text message–'Subject Letty Stark Terminated.'

Alan sat back in his chair in the real world, his mind at ease for the first time in years. The virtual world was silent, save for the faint hum of the servers. The Mind Keeper's Vault was his alone now, and he intended to keep it that way. He had rid himself of the ghosts of his past, and now he was free to shape the future.

As he twirled a pen in between his fingers, he wondered about the next chapter of his life and what could be the commercial aspects of this mind storage. The Alan Irvenko Data Storage, or Alan Irvenko Mind Repository. Or simply the initials of his name, A.I.

Meanwhile, the numbers of occupants at Care Homes decreased as the Mind Vault Storage continued to increase. Human age expectancy continued to remain static.

AI became more and more popular as the system continued to expand.

The End

◆ ◆ ◆

ABOUT THE AUTHOR

Derek Finn

Derek is a broken hearted writer with a background in pharmaceutical science, applied psychology and neuroscience. He lives in the south of Ireland and travels extensively to the Netherlands where he also has interests.

Along with his day job, Derek is also a volunteer counselor for young adults and teenagers dealing with addiction and homelessness.

BOOKS BY THIS AUTHOR

Natural Frequency

A short story comedy fantasy. This is a collection of modern life short stories told through the character of an Irish Witch and her Pigeon friend. Suitable for young adults and teenager, each short story contains a message of morality for the reader.

Wildest Moments

The second book from the frogsnotpigeons comedy series. This book follows on from Natural Frequency and tells the story of the young witch and her pigeon against the darkness of The Switchman.

Good humoured short stories with hidden message of morality.

Alice's Mind

A story of Mind and Thought Manipulation. In this novella, the stories are told from the perspective of a dream watcher who watches other people as they experience their lives. Sometimes, it crosses into inference with others through their dreams.

MIND KEEPER

Some Monsters are Real

MIND KEEPER

Made in the USA
Monee, IL
13 October 2024